CAN'T WE ALL JUST GET ALONG?

"It ain't mister, cowboy, it's marshal. You understand? Marshal Long. Don't let me hear you say it any different."

The man suddenly turned his head and spat on the floor. "Maybe we can save you some trouble. Maybe we can just take you out on the street and get you straight on this matter right now."

Longarm said, "I don't want to start at the bottom, boy. Didn't you understand me?"

The hawk-faced man swore an oath, and Longarm saw his right arm begin to move. In an instant, Longarm had his big .44-caliber revolver in his hand. He made a sweeping, slapping motion with it, catching the first cowboy on the side of the face and then continued on with the sweep, hitting the second one flush in the temple with the barrel of the gun. He dropped, joining his friend on the floor of the barroom.

Longarm's eyes swept the saloon, holding his revolver at the ready. He said, "Better nobody move or they'll be going down in a different way after which they won't be getting up. Got that understood?"

DON'T MISS THESE
ALL-ACTION WESTERN SERIES
FROM THE BERKLEY PUBLISHING GROUP

THE GUNSMITH by J. R. Roberts

Clint Adams was a legend among lawmen, outlaws, and ladies. They called him . . . the Gunsmith.

LONGARM by Tabor Evans

The popular long-running series about U.S. Deputy Marshal Long—his life, his loves, his fight for justice.

SLOCUM by Jake Logan

Today's longest-running action Western. John Slocum rides a deadly trail of hot blood and cold steel.

TABOR EVANS

LONGARM

AND THE
BOARDINGHOUSE WIDOW

JOVE BOOKS, NEW YORK

LONGARM AND THE BOARDINGHOUSE WIDOW

A Jove Book / published by arrangement with
the author

PRINTING HISTORY
Jove edition / February 1997

The Putnam Berkley World Wide Web site address is
http://www.berkley.com/berkley

ISBN: 0-515-12016-2

A JOVE BOOK®
Jove Books are published by The Berkley Publishing Group,
200 Madison Avenue, New York, New York 10016.
JOVE and the "J" design are trademarks
belonging to Jove Publications, Inc.

PRINTED IN THE UNITED STATES OF AMERICA

10 9 8 7 6 5 4 3 2 1

LONGARM

AND THE
BOARDINGHOUSE WIDOW

Chapter 1

United States Chief Marshal Billy Vail said offhandedly, "Custis, have you ever been to one of them circuses? You know, the kind that travels around with wild animal acts and all such as that?"

United States Deputy Marshal Custis Long gave his boss a wary look. A man needed to be careful before he up and answered one of Billy Vail's seemingly innocent questions. All too often, they led to long, hard assignments. It was very seldom that the chief marshal told a story for a story's sake or an anecdote to entertain one of his deputies.

Longarm said, "Well, I don't know, Billy. Yeah, I reckon I've seen a circus now and again when it was handy in what little time I have off from work."

Billy Vail said, "You ever seen that lion tamer? You know, that guy that gets into that cage with them lions and tigers all in a ball, carrying on, fussing and fighting among

1

themselves. He just gets in there with a whip and a chair and separates them. You ever seen that?''

Longarm was still cautious. He said carefully, ''Well, I might have seen something like that, Billy. Why? You got something special in mind?''

They were sitting in the chief marshal's office on the second floor of the federal building in Denver, Colorado. Billy got up from his creaky old swivel chair, walked over to the window behind him, and looked out at the weather. It was coming a good spring after a hard winter and Longarm had reflected, as he had walked over to the office from his boardinghouse, what a pleasure it was to wear an open-necked shirt and feel the pleasant breeze blowing past his skin. He had finished, not much long before, a hard trip through the mountains, through snow and ice, and through some awfully hot lead. He was looking forward to a rest in the comfort of the big city of Denver and the equally attractive charms of several lady friends of his about the town.

Billy Vail said, ''You know, that's a mighty brave fellow who walks in there and separates them lions and tigers like that.'' He turned around to look at Longarm. ''Ain't that a fact?''

Longarm had been resting his boots on an incidental chair. He took them down and set them on the floor with a clump. He leaned forward. He said, ''Billy, I'd like to remind you, I just came off a tough assignment. I damned near got frostbite, snakebite, and bullet bite, and I ain't looking to get lion or tiger bite or bit or however you want to say it. I don't know what you got in mind, but if there's some circus that needs cleaning up, then there's some deputies a hell of a lot more junior than me who can go and tend to it.''

Billy Vail shook his head slowly. He said, ''Don't you know that there is certain jobs that only a man named Longarm can do? You know, you didn't get that name on account of the way you parted your hair.''

Longarm snorted. The nickname was both a trial and a tribute to him as far as he was concerned. He supposed it came about because his last name was Long and it was known that he was the long arm of the law. No matter where you went or where you hid, eventually Custis Long was going to show up and say it was time to go to jail. Either that or boot hill.

Longarm said, ''Now, don't come with any of that foolishness on me, Billy Vail. I've been to two county fairs and a grass fire and I'm not a bit impressed with this kind of talk.''

Billy Vail said, looking sorrowful, ''Custis, I hate to ask this of you, I really do.''

Longarm snorted again. ''Why, you lying old fraud. You don't care what you ask of me. I'm surprised you let me have time to change horses before you send me out on some other damfool errand.''

Vail shook his head. He said, ''Now, you're playing me wrong, Custis. Lord have mercy, if there was another soul I could send, I'd cut off my right arm before I'd send you.''

''If I had a dollar for every time you said that, I could break the biggest poker game in the state or have the money to buy out the biggest whorehouse in New Orleans. What is it this time? And it better not involve no lions and tigers.''

''Well, we've got a situation down in Texas that is going to take some mighty delicate handling, and you're the only man I can think of that could do the job.''

Longarm sighed. He said, ''Billy, do you realize how long I was out this last time? I was out damned near two months, and I bet you there wasn't three nights out of that two months that I slept in a bed or had three meals on two consecutive days. I got rode hard and put up wet, wore out six horses,

3

damned near burned the rifling out of every pistol I own, and now you want me to off and settle some squabble down in Texas? What is it this time? Somebody discovered an honest politician and it's got them worried sick?''

Billy Vail came back around to his chair and sat down. He put both hands flat on top of his desk. He said, ''There's a little town down in the hill country of Texas, about a hundred miles out of Austin. It wasn't worth a damn ten years ago, but now that all the Indian trouble is out of there, all of a sudden they're discovering what wonderful grass there is around there and what wonderful water they have. Everybody is wanting to crowd in there, but unfortunately, there's a couple of old nester families that ain't looking for company and they're making it kind of hard on everybody, including each other. So, I need to send somebody in there that knows how to separate lions and tigers. I don't expect you to use a whip and a chair, but it ain't a job for one of the younger men, Custis. I've got to tell you that.''

Longarm sat there looking disgusted. He didn't know about the younger men. All he knew was that he felt about a hundred years old at the time. His face, from the weathering it had taken through hard usage, said forty. But the big shoulders and the muscled arms and the rest of his body said younger. He was a little over six feet tall and weighed one hundred and ninety-five pounds, mostly made up of leather and bones and sinew and muscle. He said, ''Billy, aren't you ever ashamed of yourself for the way you treat me?''

For a change, Billy Vail looked almost sympathetic. He said, ''Custis, I do hate to do this to you. If the truth be told, I really hate it. In fact, I came near to hesitating about picking you for this job, but I've got no choice. There's big trouble down there, big enough that a local congressman got involved and he went to pestering a United States congressman and the United States congressman came to the marshal

4

service in Washington and now they've contacted me and put the heavy load on my shoulders.''

Longarm looked at him disgustedly. He said, ''And naturally, you knew right where to transfer that heavy load, didn't you? Billy, if it weren't for friends like you, I couldn't afford enemies.''

Billy said, ''Now, Custis, that's no way to talk. This ought to be a pretty easy job for you. You just go down there, talk that slick talk of yours, get those folks to understand that there won't be a profit to objecting to what you have in mind, and everything will come out fine.''

Longarm sighed and looked away. He'd had a very satisfying week or two of vacation planned, most of it built around the several ladies of his close acquaintance. He said, ''How soon do you need me to go whipping off on this important mission?''

Billy Vail looked down at his desk. ''Well, I reckon you ought not try to leave tonight. I'd imagine that it might be tough to get train connections heading in that direction.''

Longarm threw his hands up in the air. He said, ''Well, you old son of a bitch, I don't believe this. And what's more, I can't see where it's any of our damned business. Sounds like to me that it's local law's business. Why doesn't the sheriff tend to it?''

''Well, this little town is set way out the hell away from nowhere and it's sitting right astride the line between two counties. One sheriff can't handle the whole mess and the other can't handle the whole mess and they can't seem to get together and cooperate.''

''What about the town marshal? Don't they have one?''

''Nope. Anybody that's smart enough for the job is smart enough not to take it.''

Longarm took his hat off and scratched his head. He said, ''Hell, Billy, what's going on down there?''

5

"There's killing going on, Custis. There's some serious trouble down there. The big problem is the new settlers that have come in there have run afoul of these two old nester families who have some big holdings around there."

"What are their names?"

"One family is named Barrett and the other . . ." He paused while he shuffled around some papers on his desk. ". . . and the other bunch is named Myers."

"Which one of them is in the right?"

Billy Vail shook his head. "Neither one of them. The problems with the newcomers is that the Barretts say that if you ain't on our side, then you're on the Myerses' side and that makes you our enemy and the Myerses say the same thing. I tell you, Custis, I think they're running out of room to bury folks. I think they're starting to have to bury them in stacks."

Longarm shook his head slowly. "Billy, you wouldn't exaggerate every now and then, would you?"

"Well, I ain't exaggerating about the pressure I got from Washington, and if I've got to have some strong words directed at me from them, then I reckon I'm going to redirect them at you. So get down there and clean that mess up. The name of the town is Grit. It's about fifty miles west of the town of Junction and about forty miles east of the town of Brady. It's beautiful country, from what I understand, unless you're six foot under it."

But Longarm was not quite ready to give up. He said, "Billy, let's don't get so damned hasty about sending me off to Texas. In the first place, why don't the famous Texas Rangers do something about this matter?"

Billy Vail shook his head. He said, "They claim to be stretched too thin with trouble along the Mexican border. But that ain't the main concern here that makes it federal business. There's squabbling about free federal government grazing land. That makes it federal business, and that makes it our business."

Longarm said, "Hell, there's government grazing land all over this country. We don't have to go down there and divvy it up. Everybody can graze on United States free land."

Billy Vail ran a hand through his thinning white hair. He looked every bit of his sixty years of age. He said, "Well, that's just it. The Barretts and the Myerses are the ones doing the deciding who's going to graze cattle on that free land. They're pretty hard-pressed to even let one another get a cow on it, much less anybody else. It's serious, Custis. I wouldn't be sending you out this quick if I really believed it didn't need tending to."

"You are telling me that there is killing going on over this matter?"

Billy Vail shrugged. "Well, that's what I've been given to understand. I don't think it's been anything big thus far, not the way I was describing it earlier. The word I get is that it's a powder keg with a lit fuse and the faster you get down there, the better off you'll be."

Longarm pulled a face. He said with disgust, "Damn it, Billy, I'm give out. I'm as tired as hell, and I deserve a little whiskey and women and some good times. I ain't taking off tomorrow and I ain't taking off the day after that. I ain't going to take off until I get good and rested."

Billy Vail looked up at Longarm, his washed-out blue eyes going hard. He said, "Naturally, I want you to be as rested as you can be, but I don't figure you need more than forty-eight hours' rest. Anybody that needs more than forty-eight hours to rest up don't need to be working for me."

Longarm stood up. He said, "All right, you old son of a bitch. One of these days, your sins will catch up to you and I'll be right there to shake hands with the devil while they shovel dirt in your face."

Billy Vail sat back in his chair. He smiled pleasantly and said, "Yeah, and from where I'll be laying, I'm not too sure I can tell which one of you will be the devil. Now, get on out of here and get some work done. Or at least let me get some work done."

Longarm put on his hat and opened the office door. He gave Billy Vail one last look and then said, "I hope you're proud of yourself, Chief Marshal William Vail. I was the only friend you ever had. I've got to tell you, I'm getting damned sick of Texas. I'm going to come back a changed man. By the way, how many guns am I going up against down there?"

The chief marshal shrugged and said, "I don't know. What do you care? Just take them on one at a time."

Longarm stared at him for a long moment and then shook his head and closed the door behind him.

A new lady boarder had moved into Longarm's boarding-house just before he had left on the long trek to track down the escaped convicts who had fled into the snowy Rocky Mountains. The young lady, who was named Betty Shaw, he guessed to be in her mid-twenties. She was a comely young thing with blond curly hair and a very interesting figure. He had not really gotten to know the young woman before he had left, so he had been surprised the night before when she had knocked on his door only an hour or so after his return from the hard trip. He had been unshaven, dirty, and generally a mess.

It had surprised him to see her standing there in a trim-fitting white gown that had displayed her hips and bosom to an appealing degree. She had come, she said, to welcome him back and to invite him to take coffee with her one evening after supper.

The somewhat forward invitation had surprised him, but

it had naturally given him a great deal of delight since Miss Shaw was quite a treat to look upon. She acted demure and modest, though Longarm sensed something more than smoke rising from the embers he detected inside her. He had been told that she had worked for a time for a tent evangelist and then, for reasons known only to herself, had left his employ as the crusade left Denver. He'd never gotten it straight what she was doing for a livelihood while she remained in Denver. But as he walked home from Billy Vail's office in the late-afternoon sunshine, he decided that it might not be a bad idea to see if the young lady would care to extend the coffee invitation for that evening.

He had planned originally to go to his oldest flame in the town, the lady dressmaker. But she, of late, had begun to hint more and more at the idea of matrimony, a subject Longarm was not too interested in discussing. Besides, Miss Betty Shaw was intriguing in her newness. The one thing that Longarm could not stand was not knowing what lay beneath the contours and materials of a pretty frock. It was like the wrapping on a present. You didn't really know how valuable the gift was until you got the decoration off.

Miss Shaw answered the door at his first knock, looking as demure and pretty as he had remembered her from the somewhat half-drunken previous night. Now, of course, he was clean-shaven and barbered and bathed and wearing better clothes. He swept off his hat at the sight of her and she smiled pleasantly. She said, "Why, Mr. Marshal Long—whatever—such a pleasure."

She had a slight southern accent and he believed that she had said, or someone else had told him, that she was from Louisiana.

Longarm said, "Miss Shaw, I beg your forgiveness for the condition in which I met you last night, but I was just back from a long and troubling job of work. I would have certainly been delighted to have taken coffee with you. I wonder if tonight, however, I might have the pleasure of your company at supper. I suggest we not dine here at the boardinghouse, but that we go to one of the finer establishments around town, of which there are several. Perhaps we could then return here and have coffee or such as you care for in your rooms.''

Her bright little face lit up and her cherry red lips opened to reveal sparkling white teeth. She said, "Oh, Marshal Long, that would be ever so pleasant. I would thoroughly enjoy that.''

Longarm said, "Well, ma'am, it's now not quite half past three. If I call for you at six, would that be convenient?''

She said, "Oh, my. Yes. Thank you ever so much. I am looking forward to a delightful evening.''

Longarm bowed slightly, backed away from her door, and then took the stairs to his second floor room. He didn't know how he had managed, but he had set the tone of the meeting on a fairly high plane. He tried to avoid doing that with women since it tended to make it more difficult to get matters down to the level he preferred. But the amenities had been observed, and he supposed that he could carry them off for a while longer. He calculated if he could get a few drinks into her, they would begin acting like a man and a woman ought to, and then he would let matters take their course. There was a chance—he had realized it on many other occasions—that sometimes, what he was there for wasn't what the female was there for, and he very often was left there when the lady wasn't.

He let himself into his room with a nagging worry. He only had a couple of nights in Denver and he had better take full advantage of them so far as the fairer sex went. He had a pretty good idea that somehow his trip to Texas wasn't going to be the kind that made pie very available. He had just gotten back from six weeks of doing without, and he was damned if he was going off someplace where the only pie to be had was apple or peach—the kind you baked in the oven.

If Miss Shaw did not show early signs of cooperation, he intended to cut her off as soon as possible and head off to his old standby, the dressmaker lady, matrimonial plans or not. He figured he could get around that and get what he was after—at least over the space of two nights. But he was not willing to walk away from such a sparkling, brand-new little heifer without at least giving her tail a little twist.

Miss Shaw had changed her blue frock for a silvery gown complete with a small hat featuring a feather and a veil. The material was light and clingy, and Longarm found occasion, on the walk to the hotel, to drop slightly behind her and admire the motion of her hips.

He took her to a downtown restaurant, one of Denver's finest. It was but a short pleasant walk in the evening air and they . arrived while it was still light. Normally, Longarm didn't eat in such expensive places, but he thought that with time being as short as it was, he'd better put on the dog if he was to impress the young Miss Shaw. They got a table and while he ordered a steak, she went in for the mountain trout and a rash of vegetables.

Longarm did not know a great deal about her career with the tent evangelist, and during dinner, he tried to draw her out on the subject. All he met with was blushes and reluctance to discuss either the tent evangelist or his work. Longarm couldn't even find out if the man represented any known denomination. The best he could gather was that he was supposed to have been some kind of faith healer who sold liniment after the show or the performance or the service, whatever it was called. Miss Shaw did admit to being one of his twelve so-called handmaidens. He didn't know what

11

that meant in evangelist talk, but he had a pretty good idea what it meant in men's talk. It made his spirits rise. He determined that in spite of the extravagant bill at the restaurant, the evening might well prove worth it.

They ended up back in Miss Shaw's rooms. By rooms, the boardinghouse meant a bedroom and a very small sitting area. Miss Shaw brewed some coffee in a big kettle on a small gas ring. Longarm would have preferred a quick shot of whiskey out of a bottle, but since Miss Shaw offered none, he didn't ask.

While they waited for the coffee to brew, Longarm probed gently at Miss Shaw's former occupation, hoping to find some clue as to her vulnerability. She had joined up with the evangelist or faith healer or liniment salesman—whatever he was—in Shreveport which was a big town near the Texas border in northern Louisiana. She admitted with a shy smile and a becoming blush to having been swept away by the gentleman's persuasiveness and enthusiasm. His name, it turned out, was Mr. Stafford. She was impressed that he took up no collection during the service and only tried to make ends meet through the sale of his wonderous liniment he sold after the meeting. The liniment was guaranteed to cure all forms of rheumatism, sore joints, aches and pains, and was even said—if taken internally in small doses—to be good for female ailments. She had blushed even deeper at the last. To Longarm, it had sounded like another snake oil sales job and made him even more interested in the delectable Miss Shaw.

Finally, the coffee was made and they sat drinking it out of cups and saucers a little too delicate for Longarm's big hands and hard fingers. Miss Shaw occupied the middle of a small settee and Longarm made himself as comfortable as he could in a straight-backed, velvet-covered sitting chair. There was a small table between them that served as a place for him to set the saucer rather than trying to juggle it along with the cup. He finished his coffee with some haste and waited patiently while Miss Shaw daintily sipped to the last of her cup. When she finally set her cup and saucer down, she looked up at him expectantly and said, "Would you care for more coffee, Marshal Long?"

Longarm shook his head, wondering what was to come next. He said, "No, ma'am. I don't reckon."

She suddenly stood up and took the step or two that lay between them. She said, her face going calm, "I'm ready now."

Longarm looked up at her, slightly startled. He said, "What? Ready for what?"

She said, "Why, for you to have the use of me."

Longarm swallowed, feeling his throat suddenly becoming swollen. He said, "Use of you?"

She nodded. She said, "Before we went to eat, I bathed real careful and washed all my parts, clean, and for the past four hours I've been thinking clean thoughts. Like you'd want."

Longarm swallowed again. A fever was starting to rise to his brain. He didn't know his part. He didn't know what to do or say. This woman was directing him, but she wasn't doing a very good job at it. He said, "Miss Betty Shaw, what do we do next?"

She looked perplexed as if she was dealing with a backward student. She said, "Why, you've got to take these clothes off me. I'm not supposed to do it."

Longarm stood up slowly. He said, "Well, yes. That would be the way of it, wouldn't it? But I don't see an opening on that dress."

She turned around, presenting him with her back. A row of buttons ran from the top of her dress down to the hem.

She said, "Well, you'll have to undo the buttons, won't you?"

With unsteady fingers, Longarm started on the first button. He said, "Well, yes, ma'am. I reckon I will."

Chapter 2

·

In the glow of the kerosene lamps, her skin shone like lightly gilded satin. Naked, she seemed much smaller, but her parts were as wonderfully placed and put together as he could have wanted. Her breasts were not large, but they were thrusting and wonderfully shaped and tipped with rouge-colored berries. The thatch that ended where her legs formed was golden and silken. She stood there, shivering slightly, even in the warmth of the room. Her clothes were piled around her on the floor. Longarm stood there, looking at her, admiring her beauty. After a moment, he put out his hand and turned her around slowly, admiring her rounded buttocks and her straight, shapely legs.

He leaned down and kissed her softly on the neck as he ran his hands all over her body. She was very still, her breathing steady. He wondered at her composure. She did not seem the slightest bit excited. Her calmness was perplexing him. He said into her ear, "What do we do now, Betty?"

Looking straight ahead, she said, "Aren't you supposed to take me into the bed? Isn't that how you make the best use of me?"

Longarm said, "Don't you want to go to the bed?"

"I just want to please you. I'm a virgin again for you. I will be whatever you want me to be."

Longarm was perplexed. It was almost as if the woman were in a trance. He guessed that it had something to do with her days with Mr. Stafford. It was the only thing he could figure, but he was damned if he would take advantage of a woman who was in a daze. He didn't know if she was really a virgin—for all he knew, she might well be. But it was not his style to take advantage of a situation where one party wasn't quite in their right mind. But then, neither was it his policy to pass up a piece of pie when it came his way.

He said, "Well, let's go into the bedroom and see what happens."

Almost as if he had started her with a spur, she stepped forward, walking past the settee, and turned right, through the door into the bedroom. She walked straight to the edge of the bed and then stopped. Behind her, Longarm was shucking his shirt and his gun belt and trying his best to get his boots off while he was still walking. It was a moment before he could get completely naked himself, but she never budged from where she was standing facing the bed.

She had left the lantern lit in the bedroom and it was impossible for him to not be wildly excited by the sight of her. She was a truly desirable young woman. His only problem was that he didn't know what to do next and he was beginning to feel like a fool having to ask her.

He said, "Miss Shaw, I think you better lay down on the bed."

"All right," she said. "On my face or on my back?"

"Let's start with you on your back with your legs spread open."

"All right." She obediently climbed up on the bed on her hands and knees until she was in the middle of the big space. She turned over and lay her head on the pillow, pulled her legs up, and opened them to reveal the golden skin running into the golden hair that turned into the soft pink of her vagina.

As Longarm climbed up on the bed, he was so aroused, he was worried that he'd be much too quick. But then, the way she was acting, he wasn't sure what was expected of him. He got down over her and said, "Miss Shaw, are you sure this is something that you want to do?"

"I'm just here for you to use. Ain't that what a vestal virgin is supposed to do?"

Longarm said, "Miss Shaw, I've never seen a vestal virgin so I don't know what they do, but I don't reckon you are one."

She said, "I can be whatever you tell me to be."

Feeling a little strange, he decided to proceed one step further. He put his mouth over hers and then guided himself into her. As he plunged his penis into her already warm and moist vagina, he felt her suddenly stir. Her mouth came open and her arms wrapped around him, clinging like iron bands. Her legs came up and before he realized it, she had exploded beneath him. The very strength of her surprised him, not just the strength of her arousal. It was all he could do to maintain his own rhythm as she pitched and writhed beneath him. But his fever was at such a pitch that try as he could, he couldn't hold back. In less than a minute, he had ignited inside her, pouring his semen into her in one great, bursting gush. For a second, he arched his back and then collapsed on top of her.

He was slightly dazed, but he was amazed to find that she had not stopped. She was still working him, clasping him by the buttocks and pulling him back and forth in her, even though his member was no longer stiff enough for the purpose. Finally, she subsided and they laid still for a moment. He gasped in her ear, "I'm sorry. Just give me a moment."

He rolled over to her side and lay on his back beside her, staring at the ceiling, panting for breath, not so much from the exertion as from the passion. But he had only a short relief before he realized what was happening; she had risen up on her knees and taken him into her mouth until she had brought him back to such a state of excitement that he could penetrate her again. This time it lasted for as long as it needed to. She went off with a high-pitched screaming wail, bucking and pitching beneath him, thrusting her hips up to his. He followed shortly thereafter, collapsing this time in real exhaustion.

Some time later, they were back in the little sitting area. They were both dressed and Miss Shaw was busy heating up the coffee. Longarm was as confused as he had been before they had gone into the bedroom. Miss Shaw was once again the demure, timid, bright-faced young woman who, as far as he knew, had been working for an evangelist. He had a lot of questions, but he didn't know how to ask them or if he should ask them or if he had the right to ask them. Certainly, he had gotten what he wanted. How she chose to give it to him really wasn't any of his business, but he couldn't help himself.

When she had served them both a cup of coffee and was seated across from him, he said, "Miss Shaw, I'm doggoned if I just ain't got to ask you a question."

She looked up at him, appearing as if she had never been closer to a bed fight than a million miles, every hair in place, her dress, her deportment, her smile, all that of which she

18

had first appeared to be. Longarm half dreamed that he had imagined it. She looked up at him and said, "And what would that be, Marshal Long?"

He said, "Well, I'm still a little confused. You know, you were talking about vestal virgins in there and some other kinds of things and I know that you worked for this Stafford fellow who you said must have been some kind of evangelist, or at least, I took it that way. Uh, Miss Shaw, there wasn't nothing religious about what was going on in there, was there? I mean . . ." He could feel himself beginning to blush. "I wouldn't have wanted to have taken advantage of you in just such a way."

She let out a tiny peal of laughter that tinkled like a bell. She said, "Oh, Marshal, how you do talk. Of course, there wasn't anything religious about that and there certainly was very little religion about Mr. Stafford. He and I had our disagreements and we parted company, but I can assure you that it had nothing to do with religion."

Longarm looked at her in puzzlement. He said, "But I can't understand what you were saying about you were there for me to use however I wanted. I never had a woman tell me anything like that. It was almost as if you were supposedly under my power or something."

She laughed again, that same tinkling bell. She said, "Oh, that was just an old trick from my former work in Shreveport."

Longarm looked at her. "And what would that have been, Miss Shaw? I take it nothing in the evangelist line."

"Well, it depends on how you look at it. I was whoring."

He was about to raise the coffee cup to his lips but quickly set it back on the table. The surprise had taken him so strongly that he had nearly dropped the dainty thing. He said, "Did I hear you right?"

"Indeed you did, Marshal. And I was very good at it. I

19

decided that you would like a nice, pure, clean, innocent young girl tonight, even younger than I am, so I decided to give it to you for a very pleasant evening—and a very good meal, I might add. Besides, you're a United States marshal.''

"United States deputy marshal,'' Longarm added quickly.

"Whatever the case may be. You're still the law.''

Longarm's head was swimming. He said, "Then, am I to understand that this evangelist business had nothing to do with you? That you didn't have a falling-out with Mr. Stafford because he was tricking people with his liniment?''

She gave him an airy wave of her hand. "Oh, my falling-out with Mr. Stafford was over the terrible way he worked the crowd. He wouldn't let me work it the way I wanted to work it. He could work a crowd up, I'll give him that. He could bring them right on up to a fever pitch, but he never did any business after that. Why, we could have done five times the money we were doing, me and the other girls. But him and that damned liniment of his, it kept getting in the way. And that old rip would drink off about half the stuff while he was making it. It was for the most part alcohol, and he couldn't fill up a bottle without drinking off a bottle.'' She waved her hand again. "No, it was time to get out of there. I figured I'd do better out on my own. A couple of other girls left him about the same time, too.''

Longarm sat there staring at her with his mouth open. He said, "Miss Shaw, I beg your pardon, but it sounds like your tent evangelist had a traveling whorehouse.''

She shrugged. "Well, for the most part, I guess you could say that, although we did sell that liniment. Mr. Stafford claimed it had all kinds of curative powers, and I guess it did. It cured him of hangover every day I knew him.''

But Longarm was still fascinated by her past performance of the evening. He said, "And all that you did, that innocent little girl business, that was just for me?''

She laughed slyly. She said, "No, not altogether just for you. I like to do it, too. It makes me feel good, you know what I mean? Gets me all kind of excited again, you know, like it was the first time. You reckon that was real wicked?"

Longarm reached into his pocket for a cigarillo as he gave the matter a moment's thought. Finally, he said, "Well, I don't know if it's wicked or not . . ." He smiled. ". . . but it sure as hell was a lot of fun." He was in no way regretting having passed up his lady dressmaker for this unknown quantity. He said, knowing he only had one more night before he had to go to Texas, "Reckon what we can do tomorrow night after supper?"

She gave him a sly smile again. She said, "Would you rather me tell you now or would you like for me to surprise you?"

Longarm lit a match with the thick nail of his thumb and put it to his cigarillo. When it was drawing good, he shook the match out and said through the cloud of smoke, "Why don't you just surprise me? A man can't have too much fun in his life."

He was already beginning to curse Billy Vail anew for what he thought he would miss on this ridiculous trip to Texas, that as far as he was concerned, was no part of his business or any part of the marshal's business. But that was Billy Vail for you. Pick the best time for the worst job.

As he rattled along on the train, he couldn't get the lovely Miss Shaw out of his mind. Again and again, her diminutive, perfect figure flashed in full form before his very eyes. He could almost see the tiny blue veins beneath the golden skin of her breasts where the skin was stretched taut by the firmness of her bosom. Nor could he forget the energy she could expend in the small space of a bed, even when he was taking up most of it. His last night had been one to remember.

Unfortunately, he didn't want to remember it, not sitting in a day coach, staring out at the Oklahoma countryside as it rushed past the window of his car. He wanted to be back in Denver, enjoying that vision in physical person, not looking at poor land and poor cattle and poor homesteads with a poor prospect ahead of possibly days and days of wheedling and cajoling and trying to make peace among a bunch of knot-heads that probably didn't have a brain between them nor the conscience of a sparrow.

His last night with the lovely Miss Shaw had been one that he was never going to forget, not only for its pleasure but for its uniqueness. She had somehow contrived to have a restaurant deliver them a full meal which she had served to him while he was in bed naked. They had alternated eating with making love. He would have never imagined that the combination would work, but it had had some unique moments.

But then, he had to leave the next day without seeing her. She asked when he would be returning, but he didn't know nor could she assure him that she would be there upon his return. She shrugged and said, "Well, I'll be here until something better comes along. I may go back to whoring, though I would rather not. I liked it better pulling a medicine show as Mr. Stafford called it. That's kind of fun, hustling them rubes."

Longarm had given her fifty dollars, not, he had assured her, in payment for her services, but just in case it might allow her to stay over a few extra days so that she would be there when he returned.

He had spent the night before in the train station in Oklahoma City, waiting to get out on an early-morning passenger train. He had brought his own horse along, a good roan gelding that had plenty of staying power and some fair speed. He figured he'd be doing a good deal of riding back

22

and forth between the warring parties, and he wanted to be able to do it in the comfort of his own saddle and on his own horse. That had caused him to pass up one connection in order to get a passenger train that was also hauling some stock and freight cars so he could bring his horse along. It was making the trip that much longer, but he figured it was worth it.

He was already bored and he was not yet twenty-four hours into the job. They would arrive in Austin, Texas, later that night and then he'd get a southbound train from Austin, getting off in Brady, and from there he would ride east toward the town of Grit.

The name of the town alone was enough to irritate him. What kind of name was that for a town? Grit? He doubted seriously it had anything to do with courage or guts or gumption. Most likely, it meant an irritant, like a grain of sand in a man's eye. Grit. What a name. He was already pretty sure he knew the people that would be there. He was pretty certain that he had met their kind in Arkansas, Louisiana, Mississippi, New Mexico, and Arizona: thick-headed, mule-mouthed, stubborn, narrow-eyed, stingy sons of bitches who thought there wasn't but one fair way, and that was their way. He thought they'd be the very kind of people he hated to deal with. They tired him out with their stubbornness. Then of course, among them, there would be several who thought they were skillful with a gun because they had once shot a jackrabbit or maybe even a broken-legged horse. Those were the kind that were the most fun. The only problem with them was how to keep from having to kill them without getting hurt yourself. Just to kill them was no trouble at all. The problem was how not to kill them.

Meanwhile, the flat, scrub-covered, brownish gray landscape unrolled outside of his coach window, while the train swayed back and forth and clicked and clanged over the rail joints. He had a bottle of his good Maryland whiskey sitting on the seat next to him, and he pulled the cork and took a hard drink. He hoped he had brought enough. He had four more bottles in his valise and a good supply of his own particular brand of cigarillos. What he was going to miss, he imagined, was some peace and quiet and some good food and some good female company. If this bunch in Grit ran true to form, not only would the men be ignorant and stubborn, but the women would be as ugly and tight as a virgin soaked in alum.

As the train rattled along, he reviewed in his mind what he knew about the situation. The Barrett family was primarily composed of three brothers, all married, who lived on separate but adjoining ranches. They had a number of cousins and uncles and other minor kin in their camp. Together, they had homesteaded twenty 160-acre homesteads for a total of 3,200 acres that they could lawfully control. The whole area, however, was right in the middle of a huge government free range reservation of better than a half million acres. It was generally considered that a man was allowed to graze on government land on the basis of 1,000 acres for each of his homesteads. That would have allowed the Barretts reasonable grazing rights to 20,000 acres plus what they owned, but of course, that would not be near enough rangeland for the amount of cattle they were running, which Billy Vail had said was around eight or nine thousand head. He had said that the Barretts were controlling upwards of 200,000 acres.

The Myerses, on the other hand, were one major family, with a father, Jake Myers, two grown sons at home, and two married sons that lived on adjoining but separate homesteads. They, along with their kin, controlled or owned twenty-two homesteads, almost the same number as the Barretts. And just like the Barretts, they took up the other half of government rangeland with their ten thousand cattle.

The best information Billy Vail had showed that there were some 50 or 60 homesteaders scattered around the area of the town of Grit, which was little more than a village of around 500 souls. According to Billy, the Myerses and the Barretts, when they weren't fighting each other, were cooperating in making life very difficult for the individual settlers, farmers or ranchers who were trying to make a living off their land and the free government land.

It seemed to Longarm that there were to be two major battles: one was to be the fight between the Barretts and Myerses for control of the whole area; the other was the fight in which the Barretts and the Myerses were both trying to drive off the small settlers. Longarm imagined there was probably also a third fight where some of the settlers were trying to band together to fight back in numbers against the two big outfits that were making life difficult for them.

He got out a folded piece of paper from his pocket and looked at it. It had the names of all the main people involved in the Myers family and the Barrett family and some of the settlers who had been doing the bulk of the complaining about the treatment they had been getting. There was a lot of names, and Longarm didn't expect to have them memorized by the time he got to Grit. Besides that, he was not planning on going into the situation with any preconceived ideas.

In the past, all too often, he'd gone into situations prepared by information he'd been furnished. All too often, that information had nearly gotten him killed. Now, he went in on a job with his eyes open and his ears open and his mind clear of any previous thoughts. He played the cards as he saw them being dealt. Anything else was foolhardy and asking for trouble.

But there were some points of the information that he

thought worthwhile to remember. On the Myers side, it was said that the old man, Jake, while not physically very threatening, was dangerous because he was treacherous and tricky and appeared to have no concern about right and wrong. He was a bushwacker and a back-shooter and was content with himself, so long as his rivals were dead and he was alive. Of his two sons, Jack and James, Jack was considered the more dangerous, but that really meant nothing since, in the flock of nephews and cousins, there were was plenty of gunhands. On the Barrett side, the three brothers were all middle-aged and not considered any more dangerous than most middle-aged men who had led hard lives in hard country growing up against hard customers. But then again, there were plenty of younger brothers and nieces and nephews and cousins to make for a fair amount of people who could operate deadly hardware with good skill.

It was interesting to note that among the settlers, a man named Tom Hunter was a stubborn and tenacious nester who had given both the Barretts and the Myerses a fair share of trouble and who, it was said, killed several of the hired hands working for both of the families. There was another family of settlers, and Longarm didn't know if it was a father and son or two brothers or an uncle and nephew. All he knew was that they had the common last name of Goodman. Their first names were Robert and Rufus. They, too, had given both of the wealthier families more trouble than they had expected.

But it didn't really make any difference to him who was skilled in the use of firearms and who wasn't; none of them were as skilled as Longarm. He was going to go down there and kick a few folks around, shoot a few if he had to, but the point was going to be made that they were going to live in peace or they were going to live in pieces. He was out of sorts and he was irritated, and he intended to complete the

26

job just as fast as he could and get back to the delights of Miss Shaw and her infinite variety of pleasures. He'd only sampled two so far, and he was eager to see just how fertile her imagination was.

The way the train was traveling, it didn't appear he was ever going to get to his destination. He was held up by a five-hour layover in Austin before he could finally get a train that could take him southward to the frontier town of Brady. But there was good news at that because they discovered that there was a rattler he could catch out of Brady that went east on a narrow-gauge track to Junction and then on down to Del Rio, down near the Mexico border. He was told that he could be put off at a siding that would be no more than five miles from the little town of Grit. He was sure that his horse was as sick of riding the train as he was.

He spent an uncomfortable night the rest of the way into Austin and then waiting for his train and the subsequent ride to the town of Brady. The rattler left at 6 A.M. and he managed to board it with his horse in a stock car without getting any breakfast. At least he had seen that the roan had feed and fresh water. The little rail banger did not have passenger coaches, so Longarm was obliged to ride in the stock car with his horse. It didn't make much difference. Longarm was already as dusty and as dirty and bewhiskered as he could get, and he didn't think the straw and dust blowing in through the slats of the stock car could get him much dirtier. Besides, his horse seemed glad of the company.

As the sun got up good, he was able to see the countryside. It was called the hill country for good reason. It was mainly comprised of low, rising mounds and sharp draws and craggy little cliffs, but it wasn't rough country in the main. Between the brown, scraggly hills were many grassy meadows and pastures. The land was cut by many swift and clear-running waterways, some creeks only a few yards across and some tumbling and cascading rivers that were not deep, but were nonetheless dangerous by the force of their current. The air was crisp and bright, and there was a good feeling to the way the sunshine filtered through the clean air. It made Longarm feel like he was back in the high country of Colorado.

The main specie of plant life seemed to be the mesquite tree, which he knew was good for fattening cattle. The mesquite put out a pod of beans and in the fall of the year when the grass was all dried up, cattle and even goats could reach up into the trees and make a meal out of the mesquite beans. They were also a sure sign that there was plenty of surface water nearby because their root systems did not run very deep. Along with the mesquite, there was the usual Texas products of stunted post oak and cedar breaks, greasewood and brambles of briars and muscadine grapevines and patches of wild plum trees. He could only hope that his job would be anywhere near as pleasant as the country was. This had been a part of Texas that he really had always preferred.

Somewhere around ten that morning, the train came to a shuddering stop and a train man came along the line and opened the stock car door and helped Longarm put a ramp in place so that he could lead his horse down. Once he had his animal on the ground, Longarm slipped on the bridle and tightened the cinch and was mounted as quickly as he could. He had been out of the saddle far too long. His rump just naturally didn't fit a chair as it did the back of a good horse. He thanked the train man for his help, flipped him a silver dollar, and then turned his horse in the direction the man had indicated led to the town of Grit.

He rode away from the tracks down a grassy little glade. Once away from the ears of the train man, he patted the roan's neck and gave him a slight nudge with the spurs and said, "Well, we might as well get on after it. It ain't going to go away by itself, so shuffle your shoes along."

Chapter 3

The village of Grit lay in the middle of a big, grassy plain, only here and there interrupted by mounds and buttes and crags and small ravines. The town itself wasn't much: two lines of buildings on each side of one street. There was a scattering of houses around the main business section, if it could be called that, but Longarm guessed that there were no more than forty or fifty structures in all. As he came into the town, he noted there were several saloons and a couple of churches, but he didn't see a school.

His first disappointment was that there was no hotel. In the end, he took a room at a large boardinghouse run by a Mrs. Judith Thompson, a handsome lady somewhere between thirty and forty years old. Aside from her looks, Longarm was struck by a certain kind of sadness about her. He would learn later that her husband had been an early victim of the land war, which had been raging for several years. The boardinghouse came equipped with a stable, but the residents were responsible for their own animals. He'd put his roan up, stored his saddle on the stall wall, got the animal some grain and hay and water, and then went to see what he could do about his own appearance.

Mrs. Thompson had no provisions for baths for her male guests. There was a windmill located out behind her barn and stables and the men were welcome to go sluice themselves off in the stream of water pouring out of the windmill and into the concrete spillway that watered her vegetable garden. A man taking a bath under such conditions was in full view of whoever cared to look his way, but Longarm didn't much care. He got some soap and his razor and a towel from Mrs. Thompson and, taking all that and a set of clean clothes, went out behind the barn to get himself to where he could stand his own company. Fortunately, it was warm enough for such an exercise, though there was still a hint of chill in the high country's May air.

He considered the discomfort well worth it after he finally made his way back into the boardinghouse, turned his dirty clothes over to Mrs. Thompson for a wash, and sat down for a late lunch with a shaven and clean skin. Aside from himself, there were only two other boarders: one was a clerk in the hardware and general mercantile in town, and the other was a drummer passing through who sold leather goods. They were both out. Aside from Mrs. Thompson and her two young daughters, Longarm had the place to himself.

He was tired from the long journey and the long nights with Miss Shaw, but he decided that he would go out that afternoon, walk around the town, and see what he could find out about the situation before he went and braced the Myerses and the Barretts. To him, it appeared to be a pretty straightforward job. You put your badge on, you loosened your gun in your holster, you went to see the people involved, and you told them in no uncertain terms what was going to be. If they didn't like it, you took it from there. He didn't plan to be diplomatic getting the job done.

Mrs. Thompson served him a lunch of pork steak, mashed turnips, and collard greens. It was a long way from being his favorite meal, but he was hungry, and he cleaned his plate with relish. After that, she brought him coffee and a piece of apple pie which was good enough to make up for the taste of the rest of the meal. He stopped Mrs. Thompson as she was about to leave the room and asked her if there was some kind of law around the town.

She stopped and looked back at him. She said, "No, just the Barretts and the Myerses and their hired killers."

Longarm had not yet told her that he was a United States deputy marshal, nor had he yet put on his badge. He put down his fork, took the badge out of his pocket, and pinned it to his shirtfront. He said, "Well, there's law here now."

For a long second, Mrs. Thompson stared at the medallion on his chest. She said softly with a touch of sorrow in her voice, "I'm afraid it comes too late for me and my children."

Longarm winced inside. It had been a foolish gesture. He had forgotten that Mrs. Thompson had been widowed by the troubles over the rangeland. He said, "I'm right sorry about your loss, ma'am, but word just now got to us, and I've been sent down to do what I can."

She came back toward him at the table. She said, "One man? You think one man is going to change what is happening here?"

Longarm said, "Well, all I can tell you, ma'am, is that I'm going to do my best."

She shook her head with a trace of bitterness and said, "You'll be like all the rest of them that have tried to help the situation. You won't last ten minutes."

Longarm smiled slowly. He said, "Well, Mrs. Thompson, I've been lasting ten minutes for about fifteen or twenty years now. I just kind of keep stretching it as much as I can."

That brought a slight smile to her face. She said, "Well, I wish you the best. You seem like a nice man. Will you be staying with me long?"

"As long as it takes to get this job done."

She nodded. "I expect then that I better increase my grocery order."

Longarm laughed. It made her smile. He noticed how pleasing her face was when she did not have the mask of sorrow. She would have been a pretty woman except for the sad way she carried herself. She had a trim and shapely figure and her hair was brown and luxuriant. Sometime, Longarm thought, he would find out exactly what had happened to her husband and maybe do something about it. But for the time being, he was just going to aim for every weak spot he could find.

He started with the saloons. It was not his customary habit to wear his badge any more than he had to; very often he left it off deliberately. He only wore it when official duty required, and this was one occasion when he wanted the word spread far and near that a deputy United States marshal was in town and intended to make his presence felt.

The first saloon he walked into was sparsely filled. There were maybe three men at the bar and a few others scattered at tables in the small room. There was a free lunch at a table at the back, and two cowhands were busy there, filling their plates with bologna and sausages and crackers and whatnot. They glanced his way as he came in and he saw that they appeared to be working cowhands in wide-brimmed hats and leather chaps. It was the kind of country where a cowboy would wear chaps to protect his legs. These men wore the narrow-legged kind, not the batwinged sort that were mostly for show.

He took note of the four or five men he could see wearing side arms that their guns were properly set up for the most part. For him, it was a bad sign. Most cowhands carried their revolvers in big holsters so they wouldn't lose them as their horses rumbled around on rough ground where they might take an upset. They weren't meant to be drawn quickly or for self-protection, but were mainly for shooting the stray rattlesnake or coyote or wolf or to fire in the face of stampeding cattle. But these men were all wearing guns like they knew how to use them.

He walked up to the bar and ordered a whiskey. Standing at the short end of the L-shaped bar, he carefully looked each man over, making sure to let each man know he was doing it. When the bartender brought his drink, Longarm said in a voice loud enough to be heard throughout the saloon, "Is there any of the Barretts' men or the Myerses' men in here?"

The bartender paused as he poured Longarm a drink. He set the bottle down and stepped back. Then he looked carefully around the room for a moment until his eyes came back to Longarm and concentrated on the badge. The bartender was a middle-aged, plump man with muttonchop whiskers. He reached up and scratched his jaw. He said, "Just who is it that's wanting to know?"

Longarm said in a hard voice, "A United States deputy marshal would be wanting to know, that's who."

The barkeep took another slow moment to look around. By now, the full attention of the bar was focused on the corner where Longarm was standing. He said, "And what would a United States deputy marshal be wanting with folks from the Barrett or the Myers outfits?"

Longarm said, still in a hard, even voice, "I don't believe that would be any of your damned business, neighbor, but if it were your business, I'd answer by saying that I'd care to have a word with them right now.''

The two men down at the free lunch counter glanced at each other. Longarm saw them hold a few whispered words. They put their plates down and started stepping in his direction. Longarm straightened slightly, but kept the corner of the bar to where it would protect his left side. They walked toward him purposefully. They were young, he reckoned, not much more than twenty-one or twenty-two. The one in the lead was a hawk-faced young man with thin lips and well set up shoulders. He was slightly in the lead, but when the two stopped, they were standing side by side. The one with the hawk face said, ''Now, who might you be?''

Longarm looked at the man for a long moment and then glanced at the other, letting them both feel the full weight of his eyes. He said, ''I might be anybody, but it happens that my name is United States Deputy Marshal Long. Either one of you work for the Myers or the Barrett outfits?''

''How come you to be wantin' to know?''

''Well, if it's any of your business, it's because I'm wanting to talk to them. Now, I can go out to their places one at a time and talk to them, or they both can come in here and see me at the same time because I'm going to tell them both the same thing. And since it's easier on me for them to come here, I figured I'd send word to them. Do you two slouches work for either outfit?''

The hawk-faced man said, ''You don't mind takin' a little somethin' on yourself, do ya, mister?''

''It ain't mister, cowboy, it's marshal. You understand? Marshal Long. Don't let me hear you say it any different.''

The man suddenly turned his head and spat on the floor. He said, ''Maybe we can save you some trouble. Maybe we can just take you out on the street and get you straight on this matter right now.''

34

Longarm said, "I don't want to start at the bottom, boy. Didn't you understand me?"

The hawk-faced man swore an oath, and Longarm saw his right arm begin to move. In an instant, Longarm had his big .44 caliber revolver in his hand. He made a sweeping, slapping motion with it, catching the first cowboy on the side of the face and then continued on with the sweep, hitting the second one flush in the temple with the barrel of the gun. The second one dropped, but the first man staggered. Longarm raised the gun over his head and whacked the cowboy over the top of his head with the barrel. He dropped, joining his friend on the floor of the barroom.

Longarm never bothered to glance down. Instead, his eyes swept the saloon, holding his revolver at the ready. He said, "Better not nobody move or they'll be going down in a different way after which they won't be getting up. Got that understood?" Still without looking around, he said to the barkeeper, "Get on around here and wake these two sleeping beauties up. I want to talk to them."

He risked a glance down at the two cowboys where they lay on the floor. The hawk-faced man had caught the brunt of the blow on his cheekbone and the corner of his eye and his nose. He was bleeding, and Longarm could already see the eye swelling shut. The other was not cut so bad, but the barrel of Longarm's gun had caught him in a tender place in the temple. It had knocked him out. The hawk-faced man was already beginning to stir.

Longarm was impressed that the blow he had given the first man over the top of the head hadn't knocked him out. It was a testimony to either the quality of the man's hat or the hardness of his head that on top of the sweeping, glancing lick, the second blow hadn't rendered him unconscious.

The bartender came around with a pitcher of water and poured it carefully on the faces of the two young men. They both came up, snorting and shaking their heads. As they came to consciousness, Longarm quickly bent down and relieved them of their side arms. He set them on the bar beside him and waited as the two young men stood up, shaking the water off their faces and the cobwebs out of their heads. Finally, the hawk-faced man got his eyes focused enough to stare at Longarm. He said, "You son of a bitch. What do you mean, whacking me like—"

He got no farther. Longarm hit him with a short, hard, driving punch full in the face. The blow knocked the man down as if he had been chopped over the head with a wagon tongue. Longarm immediately switched his eyes to the second cowboy. He said, "You want some?"

Involuntarily, the young man took a step backward and reached for his holster. He looked down. Longarm picked up the man's revolver from the top of the bar and said, "Looking for this?"

The young man said, croaking, "That's my gun. What are you doing with it?"

Longarm said, "Probably keeping you boys from getting yourselves killed. Now, when you boys get ready to talk to me, I'll be ready to listen, but I can tell you right now, neither one of you is going to win a fight, so you might as well get that out of your mind right now."

He reached down for the young man that he had just knocked down and, with a careless hand, gathered him up by the front of his shirt and jerked him to his feet. "Now, I'm going to ask you one more time. Either one of you boys work for the Myerses or the Barretts?"

The hawk-faced young man, whose face was now beginning to show the effects of the battering, shook his head to clear it. He said, "Who the hell are you, mister? What is all this about?"

Longarm said, "I'm going to try this one more time.

36

Either one of you work for either one of those outfits?''

The younger of the two said sullenly, ''We work for Mr. Barrett, if it's any of your business.''

''Which one? As I understand it, there's three brothers.''

The hawk-faced man interrupted. He said, ''You don't know much, mister. You work for one, you work for all of them. Happens that Mr. Archie Barrett gives us our riding orders, but it just as well could be Oliver or Ben.''

Longarm reached out, took him by the shoulder, and then shoved the man toward the door. He grabbed the second one and did the same. He said, ''Fine. You go tell Oliver or Archie or Ben, all or any of them, that Deputy Marshal Long wants to see the three of them here at this saloon at eleven o'clock in the morning. You better make damned sure they get the word.''

The young one turned back. ''You can't give us no orders.''

Longarm took a step forward. He said, ''You want to bet?''

The young man stood his ground stubbornly. He said, ''I ain't going nowhere without my firearm.''

''Yes you are. You're going home without your firearm. You done proved to me you can't use it. Next time you come in, you can get it, but you better be in a much better temper.''

When the two Barrett riders left and Longarm had listened to their horses riding off, disappearing in the distance, he brought his attention back to the several men left in the room. He said, ''Now, I need somebody to go out and tell old Jake Myers that I want to see him at eleven o'clock tomorrow. I got any volunteers?''

The men stared at him, but not a one spoke or moved.

Longarm said, ''You know, I'm a United States deputy marshal, and we're sitting in the United States. By law, I can delegate any one of you to go out there. I would rather get a volunteer if I could. Somebody stand up." There were four men left in the room, and they almost all stood up as one. Without a word, they headed for the door, marching between the tables in a line.

For a second, Longarm didn't realize what they were doing. Then he laughed as the last one disappeared through the door. He said, "You can run, but I'll still find you." He turned back to the bar where his drink was still waiting, untasted. He picked it up and drank off half of it. It wasn't bad whiskey for bar whiskey, but it was nowhere as good as his own Maryland whiskey.

The bartender stood there, glaring at him. Longarm said, "I guess you're all upset about me running off all your customers?"

"No, that's when I make most of my money, when the place is empty," the man said.

Longarm laughed and tossed down the rest of his drink. He said, "Well, don't feel bad. I'm fixing to go empty out the rest of the saloons in this town. You-all will be doing about the same amount of business."

He got a silver dollar out of his pocket and spun it on the bar and then pointed at the two revolvers. He said, "Don't give these guns back to those young men until tomorrow. You understand me?"

The bartender nodded. He said, "I understand what you are telling me, but I don't understand what I'm supposed to do when they come back in here demanding them."

Longarm said, "Tell them you lost them. You'll be a lot better off. They might just beat you up, but I'll damned well put you in prison. Understand?"

The bartender glowered at him. He said, "You ain't aimin' to make many friends around here, are ya?"

"If I make a single friend around here, then I won't have done my job." With that, he turned on his heel and walked through the batwing doors and out into the sunny street of the little village. Within the next hour, he had visited the other two saloons in the town. During that time, he had confiscated eight revolvers and one .32 caliber hideout gun, bloodied four faces, knocked three men out, and fired a shot into the ceiling of the biggest of the saloons, a place called the Texas Bar & Grill.

Because of the size of the place and because they did serve lunch, he decided that he would make that the official meeting place for the next morning, and he had informed two more Barrett men and four Myers men to make sure that their bosses got the word that he would be looking for them in that place and at that time and that he had better not be forced to go out and visit them. He had also incurred the wrath of two more saloon owners, since he had managed to empty both other places with the exception of a few townspeople who had been quietly having an afternoon drink.

The owner of the Texas Bar & Grill was named McAllister. He was a short, perspiring Irishman with a bald head and an apron tucked up around his chest. He said, "Damn it, Marshal. There ain't no call for all of this. I agree that there needs to be some law in this town. I'll admit that, but not at the expense of business."

Longarm had looked at the man flatly. He said, "McAllister, until I get this place settled down, there ain't going to be any business in this town. Got that? You better pass the word around to all your fellow merchants, whether they're selling horseshoe nails or shots of rotgut bourbon. Business is over with until this mess gets straightened out. If you've any influence with either the Myerses or the Barretts, you had better urge them to get in here and meet with me, because I'm not going to be in a real good humor if I have to go see them.

Supper that night was a very quiet affair at the boardinghouse. Mrs. Thompson served them roast beef with mashed potatoes and gravy and green beans. The mercantile clerk turned out to be a Mr. Sims, a quiet, middle-aged man who gave Longarm a quick shake and a nod of his head and then fell to his food. The drummer was a tall, lean man who said that he was from San Antonio. He sold custom-made saddles. He said, "We build the saddles to fit the horse and to suit the man. We build saddles for working cowboys, people who are going to be on top of a horse for fourteen, sixteen hours a day. We make the best saddle that money can buy, but we make it for a price a man can afford. I hear you caused a little trouble in town today."

Longarm was taken off guard by the man's sudden switch in topics. He said, "Well, if you call doing my job causing trouble, Mr. Hawkins, I guess you can say I did."

Mr. Hawkins took a bite of bread, chewed it, and then washed it down with coffee. He said, "I hear tell you left word that the town might as well shut down because there wouldn't be any business done until you got things settled. That about the straight of it?"

Longarm nodded. "That's about it. Anybody that comes riding in this town had better be coming to see me or coming to kill me—either talk peace or talk trouble—because he's not going to stay in town long enough to do any business. The Barretts and the Myerses are the ones that I believe I've got to influence. What do you say, Mr. Hawkins? You've been around here, according to Mrs. Thompson, for several weeks."

The skinny man nodded. He swallowed, and his Adam's apple bobbed up and down. He said, "Yep, and I've about made the acquaintance with everybody in this settlement. In fact, I was at the Barretts when two of their hired hands came riding in. One of them looked like his face had been beaten to a pulp. They claimed there was some crazy lawman in

40

town that was going to get himself killed and they were just the ones to do it.''

Longarm half smiled. He said, ''Is that a fact?''

Mr. Hawkins nodded slowly. ''Yep. They'd gone to the bunkhouse for their rifles. Mr. Archie Barrett ordered them to put their guns down and stay on the place. But Marshal, I wouldn't be surprised if you might not need a set of eyes in the back of your head here in the near future.''

''That would be the case, Mr. Hawkins, only if I planned to expose my back, which I have no plans on doing,'' Longarm said.

Mrs. Thompson came in to see if anyone needed seconds. Longarm inquired why she didn't eat with them.

She shook her head. She said, ''Oh, no. My daughters and I take our supper earlier in the kitchen. We prefer it that way.''

Longarm said, ''Makes it kind of lonely.''

She rearranged the vinegar and oil cruets on the table and said, ''Oh, I don't mind.''

''I mean lonely out here for us. We could use your company. Three old men don't have much to talk about.''

She said, ''I'll fetch in your dessert. It's apple pie again.'' With that, she left the dining room and hurried back into the kitchen.

Mr. Hawkins's eyes followed her. He said without looking at Longarm, ''A very pleasing woman, wouldn't you say, Marshal?''

Longarm nodded. ''I'd reckon, Mr. Hawkins, but I've only known her one day.''

Mr. Hawkins looked over at him. He said, ''I meant pleasing in appearance. It don't take you that long to know that, does it, Marshal?''

''No, it doesn't, Mr. Hawkins, but right now, I've got other things on my mind. Tell me what you think. Do you think the Barretts and Myerses will come in and answer my summons, or do you think I'll have to go and put them together and make it clear the fighting has to stop?''

Mr. Hawkins cleared his throat. He said, ''Marshal, I'm a man approaching fifty years old, and I've made my living by hook and by crook throughout most of the West. There's two things I won't bet on.''

Longarm said, ''And what would that be, Mr. Hawkins?''

''One is what a woman is going to do and the second is what a man is going to do.''

''That about covers it.''

By eight o'clock the next morning, Longarm was out on the street. The little village was almost deserted. There was one café besides the Texas Bar & Grill, and he looked in to see a couple of men eating breakfast. Other than those men and a few ladies in the mercantile, he saw very few customers.

About a half hour later, as he walked toward the northern end of the town, he could see a small group of horsemen riding directly toward the village. Longarm stepped quickly to the last building on the east side of the street, which was an empty storefront. There was a wooden water trough in front with a hitching rail, but the business that had once been a grocery store was now vacant and dusty. He put his back up against the wall and watched as the horsemen came in. There were three of them. He wondered, since they were coming from the north, if they were Jake Myers and his two sons, Jack and James.

As they neared, he could see they were all three of an age much too young to be either the father or his two middle-aged sons. These were either younger kinfolk or hired riders. He guessed they were from the Myers ranch because they were coming from the north, but he had no certain way of knowing.

When they were about a hundred yards off, he saw them pull their horses down from a lope to a slow trot, aiming directly toward the only street of the town. Longarm stepped across the boardwalk and leaned against the post that supported the roof of the porch that fronted the deserted grocery store. The post wasn't much protection, being only about six inches thick, but it was better than nothing.

As he watched, the horsemen separated a few yards apart. They pulled their horses down to a walk as they neared the entrance to the town. Longarm could see them looking to the left and then to the right. He stepped out from behind the post so as to make himself clearly apparent to them and to make his badge clearly visible. The minute they saw him, they stopped instantly some twenty-five yards off.

Longarm said, "You boys wouldn't be looking for a United States deputy marshal, would you?"

They were a hard-looking trio, and Longarm could tell in just one glance that the iron they used the most was a shooting iron and not a branding iron. He had a pretty good idea that if they were from Myers, the man had sent in his three toughest hombres to get rid of the problem in a hurry.

As if on order, they all three wheeled their horses to the left and started toward him at a slow walk. They were all dressed alike, wearing broad-brimmed Texas hats, leather vests, and jeans. Just from what he could see, all three were wearing cutaway holsters and all three had either a rifle or a shotgun in their saddle boots.

When they were some ten yards from him, Longarm said, "Hold it. That's close enough, boys. You can hear me from there, and I can hear you. Who you coming from?"

The one on Longarm's left, the closest one to him, leaned his forearms on the pommel of his saddle and said, "We work for Jake Myers. We came in here looking for some hombre that appears to be stirring up some trouble. Some of

43

our men rode back in last night and said there was some know-it-all lawman claiming there wasn't going to be no business done around this town and ordering—ordering mind you—Mr. Myers to come in here for a meeting. Would that be you?''

Longarm smiled thinly. He said, ''Yeah, even as long-winded as you tell it, I guess that would be me. Though it just comes down to one simple thing: I want Myers and the Barretts to be in here at eleven o'clock this morning to get the situation talked out. I hear there's been trouble around here, and I don't like trouble. Do you understand me?''

The man straightened in his saddle. ''What's this I hear about you ain't going to allow no business in this town?''

Actually, the first time Longarm had said it to the saloon keeper, it had just been a random thought that had popped into his mind. But the more he played with it, the better he liked it. It seemed to make some sense and seemed to assert his authority. He said, ''You ain't got it exactly right. What I am saying is that nobody who works for or has anything to do with either the Myers or the Barretts is going to do any business in this town. Does that make it any clearer for you, boy?''

The man swelled up. He said, ''Who the hell you think you calling 'boy' there, old man?''

Longarm smiled but without pleasure. He said, ''You want them to be your last words, boy, because if you say 'old man' again, they will be.''

The gunman said, ''You talk pretty big for one gun standing there by yourself.''

Longarm said, ''I'm not doing any more talking unless one of you three is Jake Myers and the other two are his sons. You're in the wrong place. I've declared this town off limits to any of your kind until this business gets straightened. So y'all can get yourselves on out of here.''

44

One of the other two men said, "Who's going to make us?"

Longarm said, "Well, I'm not going to make you, but if you stay, you're going to be laying in the dust of the street with a whole lot of holes in you. Do you understand what I mean by that, boy?"

The man on the end, the meanest-looking one, said, "You're ordering us out of town then, as a United States peace officer?"

"I don't feel so peaceful right now. I recommend you wheel them horses around and get the hell out of here and go back and tell your boss to get his fat ass back in here and start talking to me, because if any more of y'all show up, they'll get the same treatment you're getting."

The man looked at the other two. He said, "All right, let's go back and give the word to Mr. Myers, though I don't think he's going to care for it." With that, he urged his horse forward in a wheeling movement that brought him toward the boardwalk and the store and Longarm. It also turned the man sideways, making him a more difficult target. Just as he was opposite Longarm, he suddenly drew. Longarm saw the flash of his hand almost an instant too late. He stepped back behind the post as he drew his own revolver, dropping to one knee. He heard the crash of the man's revolver as it exploded and felt the force of the bullet as it splintered the wood of the post.

Chapter 4

Longarm realized that he'd been caught woefully off guard. Three shots crashed over his head before he was able to level down on the man closest to him. He fired and saw the slug catch the gunman high up on the shoulder of his gun hand. He saw him lurch in the saddle, twisting, turning toward Longarm. Longarm fired again, this time the bullet taking the man high up in the chest. He went over the side of his horse. The other two were already starting to spur away, firing away over the flanks of their horses. Longarm stayed down, holding his fire. They were already at a good twenty yards, which was a difficult pistol shot, even if they hadn't been riding low and at a good clip.

The noise from the shots was still echoing when he stepped down from the boardwalk in front of the store and into the dust of the street. The gunman was lying in a twisted position on his back, his revolver still attached to his hand by one finger through the trigger guard. Longarm kicked it loose, sending it skidding away in the dust. He leaned down and looked at the gunman. He was young. Longarm guessed him to be no more than twenty-five. He had been hit in the shoulder and also had a big wound in his chest. In about an hour, he would start to stiffen up.

Longarm stood up and looked around. A couple dozen curious people had come outside and were staring his way. He made a sweeping motion with his hand and everyone scuttled back indoors.

The Texas Bar & Grill was across the street and to the left. He walked slowly toward it and stepped on the boardwalk. Mr. McAllister was standing behind the batwings, so short, he could barely see over the top. Longarm stopped in front of him. He said, "Is there an undertaker in this town?"

Mr. McAllister was working a chew of tobacco in his jaw. He pushed back the batwing doors and joined Longarm on the boardwalk. He spat into the street. He said, "Don't you mean a doctor?"

Longarm said, "No, I ain't hurt at all."

McAllister turned his round face toward Longarm and smoothed his bald head. He said, "You're a pretty cool customer, ain't you, mister?"

"Not as cool as he is," Longarm said.

McAllister spat again and looked at the man lying in the street. He said, "We ain't got no proper undertaker. The barber generally will lay them out and get them ready, but I reckon Myers will be right interested in that fellow you just killed. That's one of his top hands."

Longarm said, "Then Myers is in a world of hurt if that's his top hand. If that's the best he can bring forward, he better make peace with me in a hurry. What's that man's name?"

McAllister spat again. He said, "Wilkins. Cal Wilkins. As

47

far as I know, he was about as tough an hombre as there is around here. But I see you settled his hash.''

''Well,'' Longarm said, ''you seem to be a town leader, Mr. McAllister. I'll leave it to you and the rest of the good folks to get the barber to fetch the body in and lay it out all right and proper. I'm sure Mr. Myers will be glad to pay you for the trouble.''

McAllister looked at Longarm. He said, ''Mister, why don't you get the hell out of here? You're going to put this place out of business. We're barely hanging on by our fingernails as it is.''

Longarm said, ''Funny thing about it, Mr. McAllister, I haven't heard from the Barretts and I haven't heard from the Myerses, except for this little party of gunmen. I've heard from you and a couple of other merchants, but I haven't heard from any of these homesteaders. I'm waiting to hear that they want me to leave. If they do, I just might consider it.''

As Longarm walked back to his boardinghouse, he could see curious faces wearing puzzled looks, staring at him through a variety of windows. He paid them no mind, only went up the steps and into the big, gray two-story house where Mrs. Thompson kept room and board for strangers.

He walked into the house and for a moment started to go up the stairs to his room. He didn't feel like a drink, and he didn't really want to just sit and stare out a window. Instead, he went into the dining room just off the kitchen, hoping, perhaps, that Mrs. Thompson would have some coffee left over. He sat down on one of the chairs at the table and lit a cigarillo, thinking about the young man he had just killed.

He had no feelings of guilt about it because it was his job. The three had deliberately come to town to provoke him enough to see if he could be scared or killed or run off. Now, two were on their way back to report that no such options were available to Jake Myers. He did feel sorry for the young gunman who was dumb enough or poor enough or needy enough or overly prideful enough to put himself up against a man he knew nothing about. He had come straight at Longarm like a man who was fixing to teach another man how to suck eggs, and that was an old dog that just wouldn't hunt. You just didn't go charging straight ahead into unknown situations, not unless you were awfully good. And nobody in this part of Texas working for a scrawny land and cattle baron was going to be paid enough to be that good. Only in the regard that Longarm had known that he was that much better than Cal Wilkins had he felt the slightest twinge of guilt.

At that instant, Mrs. Thompson came through the open door of the kitchen. She was carrying the coffeepot and two cups. She said, "I heard you come in. I thought maybe you'd like a cup of coffee."

Longarm said, "I'd be much obliged, ma'am."

"Do you want to drink in solitude? I was going to have a cup, but I can go back in the kitchen."

"I only drink whiskey in solitude, Mrs. Thompson. I'd be grateful for the company."

She poured them both a cup and then went back for cream and sugar. Longarm declined, but she took a little cream and two spoonfuls of sugar.

He said, "I hope the shooting didn't frighten you."

She shook her head as she stirred her coffee. "Oh, no. We've all heard plenty of shooting in this town. It's nothing new."

"The young man's name was Cal Wilkins," said Longarm. "He decided to try me. He got off three shots before I fired my first."

Mrs. Thompson continued to stir her coffee. She said, "I suppose you're luckier than most."

"Yes. As a general rule, I don't care to have anyone get off that first shot. I kind of like to reserve that for myself. Would you happen to know anything about this Cal Wilkins?"

She shrugged and smiled without humor. She said, "Cal Wilkins, Jeff Barton, Jack or James Myers, Archie or Oliver Barrett, Pete Dill, Whitey Smith." She shrugged again. "The names are the only difference. They're all the same. Men who will kill over patches of grass and ground and cattle. My husband came here trying to make this a prosperous place. He tried to make peace. He tried to bring the warring factions together. He tried to make it a settled community with a bank. A place with order. He got paid with their kind of thinking. His death was wasteful because it didn't make sense. I didn't need to know the gunman's name. I really didn't need to see his face."

Longarm said helplessly, "I'm sorry, ma'am. I know that you think the law has come way too late, but for some folks it may not have. I'm sorry about your husband. There's nothing I can do about that now. When it happened to him, and I don't know when that was, I didn't even know this place existed. Three days ago, I didn't know anything about all this. If you need help, you've got to call out before the law can help you."

She put her spoon down and looked him directly in the eye. She said, "I'm not blaming you, Marshal. I'm just talking about the way things were and are. I don't think you've got a chance here. There's too many of them."

For the first time, Longarm noticed the blue of her eyes. He said, "Yes, ma'am. I knew coming down that there was going to be a bunch of them, but it's not my job to count. That's not what I'm supposed to do. The only counting I have to do is how many cartridges are in my weapon. That makes my job real simple. That's all I've got to worry about.''

As she raised her cup, she looked him in the eye. She said, ''You're a very lucky man, Marshal. Not all of us are born fighters.''

Longarm said, ''Ma'am, I wasn't born a fighter. I'm a peace officer, a law officer. I don't fight unless I have to, and then I make sure I get the best of it because that's what the law is supposed to do.''

A grimace fluttered across her face. She said, ''Would that the law was always on time and on the right side, there would be a lot less unhappy people in this world.''

There was nothing that he could reply to that, so he simply drank his coffee and smoked his cigarillo in silence. After a moment, she took her empty cup and disappeared back into the kitchen. He still didn't know how her husband had been killed or how she came to own the two-story boardinghouse in the middle of town. He supposed either her husband had insurance or he had been able to leave her a little money. She had spoken about him trying to start a bank; perhaps he had been well-to-do. Longarm still didn't know why such a gentle woman would want to stay in such a rough area, but then that was her business.

A little before eleven, he left the boardinghouse and headed for the Texas Bar & Grill. He knew that the Myers bunch wouldn't be there, and he doubted that the Barretts would, but he was going to make sure that word got around that he was there, waiting on them.

Mr. McAllister gave him a dour expression as he entered through the swinging doors and walked up to the bar and ordered a whiskey. The portly bartender came over and poured it for him. He said, ''Marshal, you're going to have to pick up your drinking pace if you're going to make up for the amount of business you're costing me.''

51

Longarm downed half the shot before he spoke. He said, "Mr. McAllister, I ain't under no obligation to make up for your loss of business. What I'm trying to do is make it possible for everybody to do business in this area, not just them who drinks whiskey."

"The barber wants to know who's supposed to pay for that mess that he cleaned up for you," the barkeeper said.

Longarm shook his head. "I wouldn't know about that," he said. "That wasn't my mess. That man drew down on me. All I did was defend myself. As far as I'm concerned, you could have left him in the street until the moon quit coming up. However, I will step over there and give him a chit that he can send in to Washington, D.C. It might be a time before he gets paid."

McAllister gave him a look. "What would you reckon? A couple of years?"

Longarm said, "He's one of Myers's men. Why don't he apply to Myers for his money?"

McAllister didn't answer him. He was looking over Longarm's shoulder. He nodded and said, "I think you've got company."

Longarm wheeled around just as two men came through the swinging doors. They were similar to the three he had seen this morning except that one of these men was a Mexican and the other one had lost part of his ear. They came a few steps into the saloon and stopped. They looked at Longarm. One of them said, "You the one that's supposed to be the federal marshal?"

Longarm said, "My name is United States Deputy Marshal Custis Long. Are you here from Myers or from the Barretts?"

The one missing part of his ear said, "We came from Mr. Archie Barrett."

"I didn't send for two of Mr. Archie Barrett's hired guns.

I sent for Mr. Archie Barrett and his two brothers. Where the hell are they?''

Both men bristled, but nothing else happened. Behind him, Longarm heard a slight commotion. There had been two other men drinking at the bar, men he could easily identify as townspeople. He could tell that not only they, but Mc-Allister also, were getting out of the line of fire.

"What do you two boys want?" Longarm said.

The one with the half-torn ear said, "Mr. Archie sent us in here to tell you that he ain't a-comin' to where you are, and he ain't a-comin' to where you and Jake Myers is liable to be. He said, though, that if you wanted to ride out to the ranch, he'd be willing to take some time out this afternoon and talk to you."

Longarm shook his head. He said, "No, I don't reckon that'll do. Now, here's what you go back and tell Mr. Archie Barrett and Mr. Oliver Barrett and whatever the other one's name is. You tell them I'm going to wait on them tomorrow at eleven o'clock, just like I did today. And we're going to keep on doing this until my patience wears out. Then I'm going to go see them, only they ain't going to know when I'll be there. Now, can you understand that and repeat it like you had good sense?"

The two men looked at each other. The Mexican's hand hovered very near his revolver. Longarm placed his eyes on the man's hand. He said, "I sure hope your hand don't get to trembling and get any closer to the butt of that revolver than it already is, not unless you like holes in your chest."

They both visibly relaxed. The man with the torn ear shrugged. He said, "Listen, mister. We just work for wages. We're just doing what we're told. If you want trouble with Mr. Archie Barrett, good luck to you."

"Trouble ain't what I want. Peace is what I want. Now, you go back and tell him that."

Both men started forward. The one with the torn ear said, "Hell, we might as well get a drink while we're here."

Longarm put up his hand. "I thought you heard. There ain't going to be no Barretts and no Myerses doing any business in this town until this matter gets straightened out. You boys will just have to go on back thirsty."

The Mexican looked startled. He said, "Hey, choo can't make us not drink in this place. This place is for the public. We are the public. Choo don't stop me drinkin' in here."

Longarm said, "I'm going to give you until the count of three, and I'm going to count by twos, to get the hell out of here. Then I'm going to whip the hell out of both of you."

They stared at him, hesitating. Longarm was watching them close. The men wanted to do something, but they weren't sure.

The man with the torn ear said, "You got mighty high-falutin ways, mister."

Longarm said, "That's Mister Marshal to you, young 'un. Now, get both your corn bread asses out of here. Now!"

They hesitated, still, both of them unused to such treatment. Longarm straightened up and put his hand on the butt of his revolver. He said, "Two."

The men suddenly turned as if on a common impulse and went out through the door. One of them shouted back something, but Longarm couldn't make out the words. In another moment, he heard the sound of hoofbeats as they raced their horses out of town.

Longarm watched the door for another moment and then turned back to the bar and the balance of his drink. McAllister came up, his face sour. He said, "Well, you handled that mighty nicely, Marshal. You plan on putting this town in the poorhouse?"

Longarm glanced over at the two townsmen standing over in the far corner, both with an empty glass in hand. He said,

"Looks to me you're doing quite a lot of business for eleven o'clock in the morning. Hell, people ain't supposed to drink this early."

As if it had been an order, the two men quickly set their glasses down and hurried out through the front door.

McAllister shook his head. "I don't think this is legal. I've about half a mind to get off a telegram to whoever your boss is," he said.

"Well, with that half of mind, write this down. My boss's name is Billy Vail of the United States Marshal Service in Denver, Colorado. He'll get a telegram by tomorrow. You can send it and tell him exactly what I'm doing. In fact, I wish you would. He'd be proud of me."

McAllister said, "Why don't you just go to hell?"

Longarm shoved away from the bar. He flipped a silver dollar and said, "You realize that I'm more than making up for the business you're losing by the way I drink. I'll see you tomorrow."

With that, he turned and headed for the door. Behind him, he could hear McAllister cursing steadily in a low voice. It made him laugh.

Both Mr. Sims and Mr. Hawkins were there at lunch. Mrs. Thompson served them beef stew without comment and then disappeared. Longarm reflected that he had yet to catch sight of her young daughters. Mr. Sims, as he had before, just nodded and then fell upon his meal. Mr. Hawkins was wearing his normal sardonic look on his lean face. As he reached for a piece of bread, he said, "Well, Marshal, I hear you've been doing more good works among the poor and needy."

Longarm poked a fork in his stew. He said, "Well, I don't know how poor they were, but they did seem mighty needy, at least the one. He was asking for it."

Mr. Hawkins chuckled. He said, "I've got to tell you the truth, Marshal Long. I'm more than just a little glad that my business is about finished here. I'm going to be glad to be clear of this country, because I believe you're in the process of starting a prairie fire—or a fire of some kind.''

Longarm took a bite of the stew, which was delicious, and chewed slowly for a moment. After he swallowed, he said, ''Mr. Hawkins, I think you've got it wrong. I'm not the one applying the match here. Myers and the various Barretts are the ones with the torch. I'm standing here with a water bucket, in case nobody's noticed.''

Mr. Hawkins chuckled again. ''Well, what you might be overlooking, Marshal, is that there wasn't no need for water until you got here, because there wasn't no fire. So I've got to figure that you're the one with the match.''

Longarm said, ''I'm not so sure about that, Mr. Hawkins, because I haven't talked to any of the settlers. They might have a different view of the matter.''

Sims suddenly looked up from his plate and said in a high, stuttering voice, ''M-M-Marshal, I ain't one to be interfering in other folk's business but m-m-my b-b-boss over at the dry goods store is a-cussin' your name p-p-pretty hard.''

Longarm gave the man a mild look. He said, ''And why would that be, Mr. Sims?''

Sims had gotten control of his stammer. He said, ''He says you're ruining business in this town, and about another week of your kind of law and everybody is going to be broke.''

Hawkins laughed out loud. Longarm gave him a long, slow look, but it didn't stop the chuckle coming from the man. Longarm said, ''Mr. Sims, tell your boss I regret that matters are coming out the way they are, but I'm having to use stern measures. This situation didn't get this way overnight. I've come down and I found myself a town without any law and without any respect for the law, so it has become my lot to teach it in a hurry. Carry that message back to your boss.''

Hawkins wiped his mouth with one of the cloth napkins that Mrs. Thompson had provided. He said, "Marshal, all this is well and good. I'm a businessman, myself, and I appreciate business and the power of it, but I'm damned if I see what you hope to accomplish by cutting off those two families and their hired help from this town. You're not going to hurt them."

"You may have a point, Mr. Hawkins." Longarm nodded slowly. "But it's about the only thing I can think to do. The headquarters of those two ranches are miles apart. The men I want to see are miles apart, and I can't get them together. Now, perhaps I'm not creating quite as much a hardship on them as I am on the town, but eventually, I will get their attention. When their men can't come in and buy whiskey and they can't buy the supplies they need for their kitchens and their womenfolk can't come in and buy dresses and whatnot and they can't come in and buy a new shirt, maybe then it will irritate them enough to get their attention. Maybe they'll come in and try and deal with me. Like I say, it's not the best idea I've ever had, and it may not be the worst, but right now, it's the only idea I've got. If I ride out to either one of these ranches, if I go to the Myerses or the Barretts, then I put the law on a rung below them. I came in here and declared, a little quick maybe, what I was going to do and now I have to back that up. Does that answer your questions?"

Hawkins shrugged. He said, "You're robbing this train and it's your business, Marshal, not mine. Like I say, I'm going to be on that stage getting out of here tomorrow morning. I've got a pocketful of orders, and I'll just be happy to be out of this country before it blows up."

Longarm said, "You understand, it's also a way to make these settlers come in. When word gets to them that I'm keeping the Myerses and the Barretts out, then they'll feel free to come into town themselves. I've heard it said and I've read it in the reports that some of them have been afraid to come into town because of the rowdies that the Myerses and the Barretts hired that rough up their men and insult their women and turn over their wagons and whatnot. Of course, I'm planning on seeing those people this afternoon.''

Hawkins said, ''Well, I can tell you the one that you'd mainly want to see. That would be Tom Hunter. He's the one that stuck in the craw of the Barretts more than anyone else, and he's the one that would be the last to be run off his ground.''

''I intend to go see this Mr. Hunter. He was in the report that was given to me. Do you happen to know where he lives?''

Hawkins nodded. ''Right after we finish eating, I'm going to saddle up my horse and ride out close to where Tom Hunter lives. There's a sodbuster out there that needs a set of harnesses for his mules. I'm ashamed to say it, but I also deal in harness and other kinds of rigs, not just saddles, though I personally prefer to sell a man a good saddle. So, if you're willing, you and I can ride along together within a half mile of Tom Hunter's place and I can point you in that direction.''

Longarm nodded. ''You got a horse and yet you're going to be taking a stage in the morning?''

''I've got a considerable number of samples, Marshal, so I carry them on the stage and tie my horse on behind.''

''Makes sense. There is one thing that I'm mighty curious about. I understood Mrs. Thompson had two daughters. I haven't seen hide nor hair of them.''

Hawkins smiled thinly. ''I doubt that you will. I saw her early this morning getting them down to the stage stop. I understand that she's sending them to kinfolk in Austin until you're gone.''

"Until *I'm* gone?" Longarm looked startled.

Hawkins nodded again. "Yep. You don't reckon that you're the lightning rod that's attracting the lightning? The lady is showing good sense. I figure there's going to be bullets flying around your head, and I'd just as soon not be standing next you. I reckon she feels the same for her daughters."

Longarm flung his fork on his plate. He said, "Damn! Talk about feeling unwanted. Hell, I don't think I've ever been treated like this in my whole career, even by the men I was trying to hang."

Hawkins chuckled. He said, "Now you know how it feels to be a snake oil drummer. If you ain't got what they want or if what you're selling ain't what they want, it don't take very long to get unpopular. And it didn't take you very long to get unpopular."

Longarm stood up and said, "I'm going upstairs and taking a drink of my good whiskey. Knock on my door when you're ready to go."

Hawkins nodded. "I'm going to wait for dessert. Then I'll be ready to go."

Longarm raised his hand in a motion to both Sims and Hawkins and then walked out of the dining room and took the stairs up to his room in the back of the house. He let himself in and closed the door behind him. It was a spacious room with a bed on each side. There was a big window at the back, and he walked over to it and stood looking at the countryside that fell away from the town. It was beautiful country, all right. Rolling plains, grassy and gentle, except for the hillocks and hummocks and little crags and buttes that gave the countryside its name. It was rocky ground, but it was amazingly fertile. Cattle and horses both did well on the grass it grew. He expected that it was the profusion of water that made the country so valuable. It was a shame, he thought, that with plenty of it for all, there had to be such a squabble over what there was, that too few wanted too much.

But then, Hawkins had commented on that very matter. At breakfast that morning, he had advised Longarm that he was overlooking the main cause of the trouble. He had said, "Greed, Marshal. Just plain, old, simple greed. It has been in man since time immemorial, and you ain't going to get it out this trip or a thousand trips or a million trips or even a million times around the world. The Barretts are greedy and the Myerses are greedy and most of the rest of them are greedy, too. You're feeling sorry for those homesteaders, but its money to marbles that they'd be acting the same if the situation were vice versa."

Longarm poured himself out a tumbler of whiskey and sat on the bed sipping at it, thinking about his situation. Almost from the moment he had set foot in the town, he had gone along by guess and by golly. Never really having a plan, never really thinking the matter through. Well, it had worked in the past, and all he could do was hope that it would work in the future. He knew that he might have made a mistake by challenging the Myerses and the Barretts. He should have gone out to both of their places and tried to have a reasonable talk with both parties before slamming their men around and ordering them to meet him. But then, Longarm didn't know if that would have done much good. People such as these generally mistook fairness for weakness, and they would have been more than happy to have run over him roughshod. No, taken all around, he'd probably made as good a start as he could. Now the only part that was missing was to get the homesteaders' view and where they stood, what they wanted, how much trouble they were going to be, and how much trouble it would be to make them put their guns down.

He had not unpacked his valise, so he took the opportunity to take his two clean shirts out and lay them on the opposite bed along with a clean pair of jeans. Besides the extra whiskey, there was also his spare revolver, a mate to the .44 caliber that he regularly carried. The only difference between the two guns was that the second .44, even though it was of an equal barrel length, had extra grooved rifling in it that made the gun more effective at longer ranges, though neither one was very good at distances over ten yards. His derringer was in his valise. Normally, he carried it inside the big concave silver buckle that he wore on his gun belt. It fastened inside with steel clips that would keep it in place in spite of the roughest tumbling and usage. He broke it open to make sure it was loaded with the two .38 caliber shells it carried, then clicked it shut and slipped it inside the big buckle. It had saved his life many, many times and was as much a part of his equipment as anything else that he carried.

Finally, he poured himself another glass of whiskey and was drinking it down when he heard the knock on the door. He yelled, "Come in!"

The door swung open and Mr. Hawkins stood there. He had donned a well-worn frock coat and was wearing it without a tie. He had on a black, narrow-brimmed cattleman's hat that Longarm associated with short horners up in the Midwest.

Hawkins said, "Now, I reckon you want to go and see how the poor and downtrodden are living."

Longarm said, "Care for a drink of whiskey? I've got a good bottle of it here."

Hawkins, whom Longarm guessed to be anywhere between thirty and sixty, said, "No, I drank my part. I'm leaving it to the other fellow. Besides that, I understand it won't hurt you if you leave it in the bottle."

Longarm gave a disgusted snort. He said, "That's all I need for company—a reformed drunk."

Hawkins said, "We better get moving if we're going to

get anything done this afternoon. You've got to go listen to Tom Hunter's woes, and I've got to measure a span of mules for a harness. Have you ever tried to do that?''

Longarm was checking his revolver. He said, "No, I can't say that I have, Mr. Hawkins."

"It's bad enough that I'd rather go hear Tom Hunter talk. That would damned near break my heart, so you can imagine what it's like to measure mules for harnesses. They don't like it and I don't like it, but it's got to be done because the damned fool who won't quit his homestead and go to where he can make a living has got to be able to plow. Right quick, too. In fact, plowing time is right near past. If I ever knew a man who needed a new set of harnesses, it's this fellow I'm going to see. Probably have to sell it to him on credit, too.''

Longarm looked at Hawkins curiously. He said, "Mr. Hawkins, I've got the feeling that you're not near the old grump that you'd like folks to believe.''

"Let's get one thing straight here, Marshal. I may not be old, but I damned sure can claim to be a grump.''

They rode away about a half hour later, heading east over the rolling prairie. The air was sunshiny and warm and it was a pleasure to let the horses into a slow lope and feel the breeze rushing past their bodies. Hawkins was riding a surprisingly good bay mare that covered the ground easily and smoothly. The horse trader part of Longarm rose up in his gorge and he began to eye the animal with a view toward some sort of trade. The Marshal Service didn't pay well enough to suit his taste, so he supplemented it with poker and horse trading. He quickly found out that Hawkins was attached to the mare that he called Betsy and wasn't about to part with her.

They rode about four miles, and then Hawkins pulled up his mount. He pointed off to the south. He said, "There's a spread down there right toward that stand of willows that's along the creek—one of the best locations around here. That's why the Barretts are intent on running Tom Hunter off. He's got a pretty good side and limestone house. He ought to be around there working. He never leaves the place. I've got to cut up north from here. I'll see you back at the boardinghouse tonight." With that, Hawkins put his spurs to the bay mare and was soon riding away.

Longarm made sure his badge was visible and then put the gelding into a lope. After a half mile, he could see the top of the house and then after a moment, the whole place came into view. It was a neat, well set up operation with a good-sized home that must have contained four rooms. There were several outbuildings and several well-built corrals. Perhaps two or three hundred yards beyond the cluster of buildings, Longarm could see a creek lined with willows.

He slowed his horse to a walk as he approached the house. In such a place and in such circumstances, a man, especially a stranger, couldn't be too careful. When he was within fifty yards of the house, he began to sing out, calling, "Hello the house!" in a loud voice. He repeated the phrase several times and then brought his horse to a halt a good fifteen yards short of the stone and masonry residence. He sat and waited.

In a moment, he saw a movement. A man came sidling around the side of the house, a rifle in his hands. Longarm took his hands off the horn of his saddle and raised them partway in the air to show that his hands were empty. He said, "Hidee. I'm Deputy U.S. Marshal Long, looking for Tom Hunter. Just come to pay a visit."

The man stepped out into the sun and came walking forward, leaving the shadows at the side of the house. He said, "I'm Tom Hunter." He still kept his rifle at the ready.

Longarm said, "All right if I dismount?"

The man had stopped five yards short. He said, still holding the rifle, "Suit yourself, though I don't know what business you have here."

Moving as carefully as he could, Longarm put both hands on the saddle horn, swung his leg over, and then stepped to the ground. He walked forward, letting the reins of his horse drop to the ground. He stopped a few yards short of Tom Hunter, who was a young man in his early thirties. Longarm could see an intelligent face and a work-stained hat, wide shoulders with big forearms and hands. There was an honesty and assurance about the man that caused Longarm to take a quick liking to him.

He said, "Mr. Hunter, I'm not used to standing with my hands in the air. What would it take to convince you I don't mean you any harm? You can see by the badge on my chest that I'm a deputy marshal. I've come to talk to you about the situation that is going on in this area. I've been sent down by the Denver bureau of the Marshal Service."

Hunter lowered the barrel of the gun toward the ground, but he still said suspiciously, "If you've come on behalf of the Myerses or the Barretts, you can just get back on that horse and ride off. If they can't whip us by themselves, I don't see where they've got any call bringing the law in."

Longarm laughed slightly. He said, "Mr. Hunter, I'm not on anybody's side. I got sent down here to put a stop to this trouble, and that's what I intend to do. The first thing I'm going to do is find out who's causing the trouble, and then I'm going to make them quit it. Now, if it's you that's causing it, then I reckon that I'm going to have to make you quit, but if it's someone else, then rest assured, I'll be going after them."

Hunter smiled thinly. He said, "Well, Marshal, I'm not too worried about you finding out that it's been me causing the trouble. All I've tried to do is come down here and make a place for me and my family to live and prosper. Some of the other folks haven't wanted me to do that. All I've been doing is defending what is mine.''

Longarm said, "Then you have nothing to fear from me, but I would like to have a talk with you. You're the first of the homesteaders that I've had a chance to visit with.''

Hunter had hard, green eyes and he put them directly on Longarm. He said, "What about Barrett and Myers? You had a chance to talk to them?''

"They ain't been real cooperative." Longarm smiled thinly. "I sent word for them to meet me in town, but they never showed up. Sent some boys with guns they ought not to have been carrying, and I had to get stern with them, if you take my meaning.''

Hunter eyed him curiously. He said, "You say you had to get stern with them?''

"Let's just say that they ain't going to be welcome in town until this business gets settled. In fact, right now, the rule is that none of the Myerses and none of the Barretts can come into town until the big honchos come in and talk this matter over with me.''

Hunter pulled a face. He said, "Is that a fact? First I've heard of it. That's kind of an unusual step. What do the townspeople think about all that?''

Longarm said, "Might surprise you to know that they don't much care for it.''

Hunter scratched his jaw. He said, "I've got some coffee in the house that's been on the stove since about six this morning. It could probably walk on its own legs. You want to take a chance on a cup?''

Longarm reached for the boot of his saddlebags behind his horse and pulled out a bottle of whiskey. He said, "We might could thin it down with some of this.''

Tom Hunter looked up at the sun. He said, "That might

not be too bad of an idea. Normally, it would be too early for me, but this is Tuesday.''

''No,'' Longarm said. ''I think it's Wednesday.''

''Well, either way, Tuesdays or Wednesdays are my days to drink early.''

Longarm laughed and they walked into the cool, dim house.

Chapter 5

They sat at a handmade table in the spacious kitchen of the cool house. Tom Hunter had told Longarm that with the help of two Mexicans, he had built the place himself. He said, "Marshal, I quarried this limestone out of the ground, transported it, mixed the mortar, trucked in the lumber on a box wagon, and built it from the ground up. I put in the plumbing so I could have indoor running water coming in from that windmill out yonder in the backyard. My wife could stand right there at that kitchen sink and pump that handle and get water without having to carry it in here in a bucket. I've got good barns, I've got good corrals, and I've got some good stock. Ain't none of it worth a damned to me because of Jake Myers and Archie Barrett and that bunch. I started out with a hundred head of cattle and twenty horses. Now I'm down to ten head of breeding stock and five horses. On top of that, I can't go further because I'm cut off from water."

Longarm raised up slightly and looked out the back window. He said, "Mr. Hunter, I can see what appears to be a pretty good stream from here. At least, according to that line of willows."

Tom Hunter made a snorting sound. He said, "Yeah, at one time, that was a pretty good stream, and I could water a lot of stock from it and at least part of it's on my land. But the Barretts dammed it up about five miles upstream. They've got themselves a nice lake—on government land I might add—but I don't get a drop. I have to drive my cattle to water every day and then drive them back. It's a four mile going and a four mile coming. I can't let them drift down there, or I'd never see them again. And my windmill dried up."

Longarm took a sip of his coffee. He said, "I don't understand, Mr. Hunter, why you and the rest of the homesteaders let this matter get so out of hand. From what I understand, there's about fifty homesteads around here."

Hunter nodded. He said, "Yeah, you'd think we could have handled it that way. The only problem with that, Marshal, is that out of that fifty or so men, there's only about twenty of them that's willing to fight. The Myerses and the Barretts together could double that with gunhands. But that ain't the big problem. The biggest problem is that we're isolated. We're four and five miles apart, some of us even farther. What happens when a crowd of them ride up in your front yard and go to shooting in the windows and you've got your wife and children under the beds, hiding, and you're only one gun by yourself? What do you do then, Marshal? You do what a lot of them have done. You take what they'll let you have or else you load the wagon and leave. I reckon we've lost maybe twenty families in the past year or two."

Longarm adjusted his hat and grimaced. He said, "I see what you mean. They're organized, and you're not."

"And there's not a hell of a lot we can do about it. I'm holding on here by the skin of my teeth. I'm doing it more out of plain old stubbornness than anything else. I've sent my wife and kids back to Junction where we came from. She's gone back to teaching school and I go in and get what little groceries I need about every two weeks. I don't know why I don't just give up."

Longarm looked around. He said, "Probably because this is yours, and nobody is supposed to be able to force you to give it up."

"Marshal, I can build a house, I can build a barn, I can train a horse, I can farm, I can run cattle, I can shoot, I can help my neighbor, and I can damn near deliver a baby, but I can't fight the odds I'm up against now. I can make a living back in Junction, but I don't want to work for the other man. I want my own place, and this is it. Right now, I've been thinking mighty hard about just riding into Barrett's place and calling him out. I'm not that good of a pistol shot, and there's a good chance that he'd kill me, but that's the way I feel right now."

Longarm shook his head. He said, "No, Mr. Hunter, you don't want to be doing that. In the first place, from what I understand, Mr. Archie Barrett is not the kind that's going to be called out into a fair fight. You'd be dead before you got to within a half mile of him. This is my kind of work. I can't build a house, I can't run cattle, and I can't farm, but I can take care of folks that are making other people's lives not so good. You're going to have to leave this one to me."

Tom Hunter sipped at his coffee and looked doleful. He said, "Well, Marshal, I wish you luck. I would point out that there's just one of you, but I reckon you already know that. Something is going to have to happen pretty soon. There's too many like me, barely getting by from day to day. Some of them have made their peace with the Myerses and the

Barretts, and they just stick to their own homesteads, but they can't make a living off of what little land they hold in deed. They have to use the government land, and they ain't allowed to. It's just simple arithmetic. You need so many acres and so much water for every head of stock you've got, and when the government said 160 acres was a homestead, they were thinking of raising corn. I know they weren't thinking about raising half-wild longhorn crosses. Hell, even purebred cattle would have a tough time rustling it out on what little land we have here. I've got three homesteads—480 acres—one in my name, one in my brother's name, and one in my oldest boy's name. Of course, he's only six. I hear tell that Barrett is going to challenge a lot of our claims like the one that I got in my boy's name and the one I got in my brother's name. Man, you know the law. A man's supposed to prove up his own claim. Well, hell, I could prove up 480 acres myself. I can work that much myself, but that ain't what the law says. So, I guess if they wanted to, they could go to Austin with their money and their lawyers and the next thing we'd know, we'd be getting chucked off our own land because damned near every settler around here is just like me. We've got three or four homesteads in different names. Hell, we've got to. Of course, the Myerses and the Barretts ain't no different. I wouldn't be surprised if they didn't even have some in the name of some of their dead relatives, but there's nobody that is going to challenge them at the land department.'' He shook his head. ''We're just the little fellows, Marshal. All we can do is hang on and fight.''

Longarm said, ''Is it mainly the Barretts deviling you the worst?''

Hunter nodded. ''Yeah, but that's just because of where I'm located. I'm nearer to them. They're about four miles to the southwest of me and the Myerses are six or seven miles in the other direction. I think they kind of split it up amongst themselves. I'm sure you knew that before we came in here to settle they were doing a pretty good job of having a feud between themselves. They'll probably go back to it, once they get us all run off. But right now, we're the live meat.''

Longarm leaned back in his chair and looked up at the ceiling for a moment. He said, "How many good men are there in this valley? How many settlers could I count on for gunhands?"

Hunter frowned. He said, shaking his head slowly. "Not many, Marshal Long. There's the Goodmans—a father and son—on the other side of town, about eight or nine miles west of here. He's a tough old bird of about forty or forty-five, and his son is about twenty-five. They're both tough. They're holding off Myers and his crew. In fact, I've heard they've killed several of them. Then there's a man named Swanson. He's got a brother and a cousin with him. Most everybody has sent their women away, and those that haven't, have made their peace and are sticking to their own ground.''

"Mainly, what do they do to you? Kill your cattle?"

Hunter made a face. "Oh, they kill them, they run them off, they steal them, or they beef one out if they feel like having a barbecue. Like I say, I'm down to ten, and I keep pretty close tabs on them. Of course, I've already told you that they dammed up that stream. Now, there's plenty of water around here and if I could let my cattle roam free, they could get to water. I think there ought to be some kind of law against damming up a public stream like that.''

Longarm said, "You can't dam a stream that crosses a county line where the stream is being used downstream. You can't dam it up for your own purposes. That's against the law. You can break that dam down anytime you want."

Tom Hunter laughed without humor. "Yeah, and get shot three or four times for my troubles. They've got a couple of men guarding that thing. But how come you're asking me about how many guns you can count on? You thinking about maybe deputizing some folks and taking them on?''

Longarm shook his head. He said, ''No, not right yet. To tell you the truth, Mr. Hunter, I'm still seeking information. I don't know yet how to proceed. I was told that you were a steady man with a good head on your shoulders, and I came out to get some information from you. I wish I could say that I had a plan right now that would offer you some help in a hurry, but I don't.''

Tom Hunter said, ''I appreciate your honesty, but quite frankly, if I don't get some help right quick, I'm not going to last.''

Longarm stood up. He said, ''Well, I need to be getting back to town. I've got business there, or rather, I've got business to keep out of town.'' He smiled. ''I don't want the Myerses or the Barretts to be buying anything in town. I've made it clear that their money is no good in town.''

Tom Hunter cocked his head. ''You're kidding.''

Longarm said, ''No, I'm not, and they've already found that out. I need to get back there and see if I've stirred anything up.''

Hunter walked outside with him and shook Longarm's hand. He said, ''I appreciate you coming out, Marshal. I'd appreciate hearing about anything that's coming up. If I can be of any help, I'd sure be more than willing.''

Longarm nodded and mounted. As he wheeled his horse, he said, ''You'll be hearing from me. Keep your rifle loaded, Mr. Hunter, and sleep light.'' He put his spurs to the horse and loped away from the lonely cabin out onto the rolling prairie.

Chapter 6

Longarm was waiting in the parlor of Mrs. Thompson's boardinghouse when Mr. Hawkins finally came in. It was late in the afternoon, almost half past four. He had been sitting in a big easy chair with a glass and a bottle of his good Maryland whiskey, sipping slowly and smoking cigarillos and thinking. He had a kind of hazy plan. It wasn't very good, and he didn't know if it would work or if he could get anybody to help him, but it was the only plan he had. He thought he might as well give it a try.

He heard Hawkins come in the front door and hollered at him to step into the parlor. The tall, gaunt man came in through the double doors and stopped. He said, "Well, Marshal, you seem to be taking your ease. You have a good talk with Tom Hunter?"

"Yeah, I just got through talking to a man who needs help from the law, and I'm not sure the law has any way to help him. It's a damned frustrating feeling, Mr. Hawkins. By the way, you never have told me what your first name is. Mine's Custis.''

Hawkins took off his hat and laid it on the table and sat down in a straight-backed chair. "Well, I'm not too prompt about flinging my first name around, but if it's got to be told, it's George. The second one's worse, so I don't use that one at all. Generally, I just go by G. W. Hawkins.''

Longarm smiled. "So, it's George Washington Hawkins, is it? I take it that either your daddy or your mother was a historian or a patriot?''

Hawkins blushed slightly beneath his weathered skin. He said, "Hell, Marshal, you weren't supposed to figure that one out.''

Longarm said, "Well, I'd offer you a drink, but you don't drink.''

Hawkins said, "Oh, I still drink. I just don't ever do it right now.''

"I take it by that you mean any right now.''

Hawkins smiled. He said, "That's about the size of it, sir.''

Longarm was silent for a moment, sipping at his drink and staring at the man. He liked him, liked his sense of humor, and liked his straightforwardness. He hated to play the trick on the man that he was going to play, but he didn't see any way around it. He said, "Tell me, Mr. Hawkins, who are you the closest to—the head of the Barrett family or the head of the Myers?''

Hawkins pulled a face. He said, "I don't reckon you'd say that I was invited to Christmas dinner at either place, but I reckon if it came down to that or drowning, I reckon I'd say I know Archie Barrett better. We're more the same age. Hell, Jake Myers is upwards of sixty and mean as a rattlesnake with a sore on his tail. Barrett is not the best company in the world, but I've been doing business with his outfit for ten, twelve years. I guess I could say that I know him better.''

"Well, tell me this. Would he accompany you somewhere?''

Hawkins gave Longarm a puzzled look. "Accompany me somewhere? Why would he want to accompany me anywhere?''

Longarm said, "Well, let's just say that you had a particular piece of goods that you wanted him to see, but you couldn't bring it to him. Would he come with you to look at it?''

"Like what?''

"Well, let's say like a silver-mounted saddle, for instance. A really first-class piece of goods.''

Hawkins frowned. "Archie Barrett has already got a silver-mounted saddle.''

"All right, a gold-mounted saddle, then, with diamonds or something. I don't care, just something in your line of work that a man couldn't pass up if he had plenty of money.''

Hawkins shrugged. He said, "I suppose so, though I can't figure out why I couldn't take it out and show it to him.''

Longarm said, "Let's say it was just one of a kind and it was passing through town and wasn't going to be here but one day and you'd like to show it to him. It's just one of a kind that your company made and you couldn't take it off the stage. You say you're leaving on the stage tomorrow? Let's pretend it's coming on the stage in the morning. Do you think you could get him to come into town and look at it?''

Hawkins shook his head slowly. "That would have to be some hellacious saddle. I don't even know if I could invent one in my mind that would persuade Archie Barrett to ride in here to look at a saddle. Besides that, you're supposed to have this town hemmed off from him. You've got a fence

75

out there that says No Barretts and No Myerses.''

Longarm leaned back in his chair. ''That ought to be a good selling point for you. He'd have to admit in front of you and everybody else that he was scared to come into town because of me, wouldn't he?''

Hawkins looked off for a moment. He said, ''I suppose so, though I don't know what you're getting at here, Marshal. I ain't riding out to see Archie Barrett. Do you want me to write a note or something like that?''

Longarm cleared his throat and took a sip of whiskey. ''No, I had something else in mind. Something that would be more handy, more efficient, more lawlike.''

George Hawkins gave him a suspicious look. He said, ''And what would that be, Marshal Long?''

Longarm cleared his throat again. He said, ''George Washington Hawkins, by the power vested in me by the Marshal's Service of The United States Government of America, I hereby deputize you as a temporary deputy in the service of law and order in and for these United States of America. Say, 'I do.' ''

Hawkins's mouth fell open. He said, ''What?''

Longarm said, ''Say, 'I do,' or 'I agree,' or 'OK' or something. Just say yes.''

Hawkins pulled his head back. ''Like hell I will. You're not going to deputize me as any United States marshal deputy, temporary or otherwise.''

Longarm said, ''Those aren't even the right words. It's been so long since I've done it, I forgot the right word. You're an auxiliary United States deputy marshal. And whether you say I do or you don't, you have to do it.''

Hawkins said, ''Like hell I do.''

Longarm said, ''I am duly constituted by my authority, which goes directly to the executive branch of this government, to requisition anything, man, woman, child, mule, marbles, wagons, cannon, whatever I need for the performance of my duty. And I happen to need you for the performance of my duty. So, Mr. Hawkins, you are now an auxiliary United States deputy marshal. Do you want to make it an amiable connection so you can get paid by saying 'I do,' or do you want to do it to where I've got to force you? Then you don't get no pay, no benefits, no thanks from your country.''

Hawkins's face was set. He said, ''Do you know what you're asking me to do? I don't want to get mixed up in this mess. Hell, them folks are using real bullets, Marshal. I don't want one of them things passing through my body.''

Longarm said as kindly as he could, ''George, you ain't got no choice. I need somebody to run an errand for me, and you're the only one I know that can do it. Now, you're going to have to do it, or I'm going to have to put you in jail. Which would you rather have?''

Hawkins sputtered for a moment. He said, ''You . . . you can't put me in jail. Hell, they ain't even got a jail in this town.''

Longarm shook his head sadly. ''I know that, Mr. Hawkins, but there's plenty of jails around here, and don't think I won't take you to where there is a jail and put you in it and keep you there for quite a while.''

''What in the hell are you pulling on me?''

''George, I don't have any choice. If I thought I was putting you in any danger, I wouldn't do it. All I need you to do is a simple errand for me and then you're out of it and you can go on your way. It will just delay you one day, that's all.''

Hawkins stared at him for a long moment, his chest heaving. He looked angry, and when he opened his mouth he sounded angrier. He said, ''Damn it, Marshal Long. There ought to be a law against this. You can't just up and grab a

United States citizen and make them do what you say. Why, that's the damnedest thing I've ever heard.''

Longarm nodded. ''I agree with you. It's a shame the amount of power that the government puts in a person like me. I ain't worthy of it. I ain't to be trusted with it. Here's a good example of it right here. I'm taking advantage of you, and I ought not be doing it. A better man than I am wouldn't be doing it, but I've just got to, because it's the only way I can figure out how to get this job done. If there was a better man sitting here, he'd figure a better way to do the job and wouldn't need to bother you. But there it is, Mr. Hawkins. You can see for yourself I'm not all that smart, so that's how come I've got to make use of you. I'm sorry for that, and I'm sorry for you. I'll ask you again. Do you want to agree to this and get paid for it and get all the credit and the decorations and the thanks of a grateful government, or do you want to be pressed into service and get paid nothing?''

Hawkins glared at him. ''What the hell does this job pay?''

''Two dollars a day; you furnish your own horse and cartridges.''

Hawkins stared at him. He said, ''Two dollars a day? I eat more than two dollars a day.''

Longarm nodded sympathetically. He said, ''Yeah, the damned government is cheap as hell. I couldn't agree more with you. Well, what'll it be? A good snappy I agree, I do, or what?''

Hawkins sighed and sat back in his chair. He said, ''You're the damnedest son of a bitch that I've ever run into in my life. All right. OK. I agree. I do. Whatever. Son of a bitch, now I'm a law officer.''

Longarm half smiled and lifted his glass in a toast. He said, ''That you are, George. That you are.''

Hawkins sat contemplating Longarm for a moment. ''You

78

ain't told me yet the details about what I'm going to do or how I'm going to do it."

"Well, the reason for that is right now, I don't know."

Hawkins got a strangled look on his face. "You mean that you're setting me up for something that you ain't even sure of? That you don't even know the particulars of? That you don't know the outcome of?"

Longarm laughed. "Oh, hell. I seldom know how things are going to come out. I generally just stir things around with a stick until I get the pot to boiling and see what pops out."

Hawkins shook his head. He pointed a bony finger at Longarm. He said, "Marshal, I want you to get one thing straight. I'm fifty years old, and I have every intention of turning fifty-one. You better not interfere with that plan."

Longarm said with amusement in his voice, "Mr. Hawkins, it is my intention that we both grow older. The only reason I can't lay the log to this plan is that it's still kind of flitting around in my mind. I'll have it worked out by after supper tonight and then you and I can sit in here or set out for a walk and have a talk about it."

Hawkins eyed Longarm narrowly. He said, "You know, something is starting to come back to me. Your last name is Long and you're a United States Marshal. There's supposed to be some famous old boy named Longarm. That wouldn't by some chance be you, would it? The long arm of the law? The man that no criminal can get away from? No thief, no outlaw, no murderer?"

Longarm said, "Well, I get called that mostly by people who I take to be joking. It got stuck on me some years back and it's kind of hung on."

Hawkins straightened up in his chair. "Why, you're give out to be wild as hell. They say you're crazy. They say you'll do anything. Here I am mixed up with . . . Good lord, what have I got myself into?"

Longarm held up a pacifying hand. He said, "Oh, hell, Mr. Hawkins. It ain't all that bad. You know how these stories get spread around and how they grow and get exaggerated. I'm just a peaceful law officer."

"Yes, but you're supposed to have pulled some kind of stunts. It's said that you've run men all over the country, that you never give up, that you're crazy."

"OK, I suppose that might be true, Mr. Hawkins, but don't let that be of concern to you. It just means to you that I'm trying to give you, a taxpayer, your money's worth."

Hawkins set his mouth in a grim line. "How about I don't do what you tell me to do? What happens then?"

Longarm said gently, "You took the oath, George. You don't have a choice."

"Yeah, but what if I don't really go through with it? What if I just go on about my business and head for my next stop?"

Longarm said levelly, "Then I'd make that next stop Kansas. Leavenworth, Kansas. That's where the federal penitentiary is, George, and that's where you'd be headed sooner or later."

"You mean you'd keep coming after me just over a piddling thing like this?"

Longarm chuckled. He said, "Well, George, if you let the little matters slide, then all of a sudden you've got a mountain of trouble. No, I think I can depend on you."

"And I'm supposed to be going to interest Archie Barrett in a saddle? I'm supposed to talk him into coming to town to view a saddle? You know, that's going to have to be one hell of a saddle. Hell, I can't even think of one that would interest him. He's a rich man. He's already got most of what he wants."

Longarm yawned. He said, "George, let's give it up for now and talk about it after supper. What do you think of that? I think I might even go upstairs and rest my weary bones."

"I guess I'll do the same. I'm going to need all the rest I can get."

As they stood up, Longarm said, "By the way, do you happen to know the story on Mrs. Thompson's husband and what happened to him?"

Hawkins's face darkened. He said, "Yes, and it's a sad chapter, too. It almost makes me hate to do business with either the Barretts or the Myerses. In fact, maybe that's the reason I'm agreeing to help you. He was a fine fellow. His name was Milton Thompson."

"Maybe tonight you can tell me about him."

Hawkins nodded, and then they went their separate ways to their separate bedrooms.

Instead of lying down for a nap, Longarm sat in a chair, staring out the east window of his room, with a glass of whiskey in one hand and a cigarillo in the other. He was staring out toward where he had ridden earlier to visit Tom Hunter. He was trying to work out the details of a plan that was still very hazy in his mind. All he knew was that a frontal attack on the Barretts and the Myerses wasn't going to work. They had too many guns. He somehow had to cut the leaders out and put them under his thumb and find some way to force them to obey the law. He didn't have any idea how he was going to do that, and he didn't have any idea if he could do it. But one thing he did know for certain: he was going to need a fort of some kind. A fort, a jail, a hideout, a prison. Something along that order.

He looked at his watch. It was going on four o'clock. There was still plenty of time before supper. Without thinking too much about it, he went down the stairs in a hurry and saddled his horse and rode rapidly toward Tom Hunter's ranch.

• • •

Tom Hunter was flabbergasted and surprised and more than a little doubtful after Longarm finished explaining his plan— or the parts of his plan that he knew enough about to explain. When he had ridden up, Hunter had been having an early supper of beans and bacon and corn bread, but he had put that aside to talk with Longarm. They went outside and stood under the only sizable oak tree for as far as the eye could see.

Longarm said, "Look, I know it might not work, and I know it's dangerous, and I know it's risky, and I know that there's a lot of reasons not to try it. But it's the only thing I can think of. I've got to have your help, and I've got to use your place. I know that puts you at risk. I do understand what I'm asking of you."

Hunter shrugged. He said, "Hell, I don't see what I've got to lose. I'm about finished now, and if I've got to eat my cooking much longer, I'm going to starve to death. I miss my wife. I miss my kids. I can't hold on here much longer. Yeah, hell yeah. I'm willing to try."

Longarm looked back at Hunter's cabin. He said, "Your place is ideal because it's stone and concrete. It'll make an ideal defensive position. It's also cleared all around for a good hundred yards in every direction, so it's not the kind of place that anyone can sneak up on. But if we get located before we're ready and before we've got our deals made, we're going to be in a lot of hot water. There's going to be a lot of lead coming through those windows and those doors."

Hunter shrugged. "Yeah, and there's going to be a lot of lead going back, if I have anything to say in the matter."

"The problem is, Tom, you and I can't do it by ourselves. We need more help. What do you think about the Good-

82

mans? Do you think they'd leave their place and come over here and stay for that time period?''

Hunter shrugged. ''I can't answer for them, but my guess is that yeah, they would. They ain't got much left to lose, either.''

Longarm said, ''But they'd be leaving their place unprotected, and there's no telling what could happen to it.''

Hunter smiled. He said, ''They're about burned out now. They don't have a barn left and about half their house was burned down. They're the same as sleeping outside right now.''

''What about their stock?''

''Well, what little they have left, they could drive them over here and throw them in with mine. One of us could day herd them and then put them up in my corrals at night. They'd be a hell of a lot safer than they are right now. If we don't hurry up and get the mess straightened out, there's not much left for any of us here.''

Longarm said, ''Can you think of anybody else that might be of some help?''

Hunter shook his head. ''Oh, there's a few good men left among the settlers. In fact, that's about the only ones that are left. The rest have turned tail and run. But let me ask you this, Marshal. Ain't we better off being as secret as we can?''

Longarm nodded. He said, ''Yeah, I think you're right. We'll just keep it to you and the Goodmans. What are their first names? Robert and Rufus?''

''Yeah, they answer to those.''

''How do we get in touch with them? To tell you the truth, I'd rather not be seen going over there.''

Hunter nodded. ''That would be the best part of your idea. Now, you're talking about this happening tomorrow afternoon sometime?''

Longarm said, "If I can make it happen, that's when it's going to start. But you have to understand, I can't guarantee anything. I'm guessing and gambling like I've never guessed and gambled before."

"Then I reckon I'd better ride over there tonight and see if I can't get them headed this way. I can't tell you for certain that they'll go along with it, but I'm willing to bet they will. It's a chance, Marshal, and that's all any of us are looking for."

Longarm put out his hand. He said, "Well, here's luck."

They shook hands, and Longarm walked to his horse and mounted. He said, "Don't look for me until you see me coming, and if you see me coming, odds are I'm going to be fetching you some company. I'll see about laying in a supply of groceries and whatever else we'll need."

"We're going to need cartridges," said Tom Hunter.

"What size you take?"

"Some .44s will do me all around."

Longarm nodded. "Same for me. What about the Goodmans?"

"I'll find out tonight."

Longarm said, "Are you planning on getting them started tonight?"

"If they will," Hunter said.

Longarm nodded again. "Here's hoping that I'll see you tomorrow afternoon." He put the spurs to his horse and headed down the gentle slope that led away from the cabin.

In spite of pushing his horse on the return trip, he was late for supper. The other two boarders had finished and gone to their rooms. Mrs. Thompson served him ham with sweet potatoes and rice and gravy. He asked her to sit with him while he ate. She got herself a cup of coffee and sat down at the far end of the table. Once again, he noticed how graceful and elegant she was, and except for the sadness around her eyes, her face would have been very attractive. He was eager to know what had happened to her husband, but he preferred to wait and let Mr. Hawkins tell him the story.

For a few moments, Longarm tried small talk, asking her where she was from before they had come to the town of Grit and to the hill country since she didn't sound so much like a Texan. She was from Kentucky, she and her husband both, and they had come to Texas, first to San Antonio and then to Austin, where her husband had been involved in commerce and then in the wholesale livestock business and then the banking business.

He could see that she did not care to talk about her husband's past, so he tried to turn the conversation more toward her. She had been a schoolteacher at one time and then had worked in a ladies' millinery shop. He badly wanted to mention about her sending her two daughters off, but he figured the subject wouldn't be welcomed, so he stayed away from that also. It seemed that with Mrs. Thompson there were too many subjects that were too painful to bring up. It made him feel sad and it made him feel angry. One thing he did manage to ask her was how she ran a boardinghouse with only two boarders.

She sighed and said, "Well, up until about a few weeks ago, I had five boarders, counting Mr. Hawkins, who is almost a regular since he's through here so often. But then the feed store got taken over by the Myerses, and they fired the three men who were working there that had been boarding with me."

Longarm looked down the table at her. He said, "It seems like these folks intend to take over the whole town. I've noticed a couple, three empty stores around here."

She picked at the tablecloth and looked down. She said, "I would imagine that their intention was to run everyone off from here and close everything down, except for the saloons where their cowhands can chase their whores and drink their whiskey.''

Longarm looked up in some surprise. He said, "They got whorehouses in this town?''

Mrs. Thompson nodded. "Of course, Marshal. I'm surprised you're that naive. There's one over every saloon.''

Longarm was amused. "Well, I reckon if you're going to keep the kind of hired help that the Barretts and the Myerses keep, you're going to have to let them have some recreation.''

"That's my point. I would expect that their intentions, once they get through dividing this country up, is that there not be anything here that doesn't support a head of beef or a cowboy that tends to that beef. I don't believe that they intend for this to be a town with schools for children, or churchgoing people, or banks. They want to be able to control everything, and I don't believe they'll be happy until they do.''

Longarm looked down at his plate. He said, "Well, this is none of my business, but since Mr. Sims is your only star boarder, how can you make it here?''

She said, "I can't, Marshal. I'm already making plans to move to my sister's home in Austin. You probably know that my children are already there and you're probably thinking that I sent them because your coming was going to cause trouble.''

"Did you?''

She gave him a look. "Of course. If they were your children, would you want them here in the middle of a gunfight? You're down here to stop the Barretts and the Myerses. I think there'll be a lot of trouble while you try, and I think a lot of people are going to be hurt. I didn't want my daughters to be caught in the crossfire.''

Longarm nodded. "Can't much blame you for that, Mrs.

Thompson. When are you thinking about pulling up stakes?"

She smiled and it was a delight to see. She said, "I suppose when you leave. I've got a grandstand seat, and I don't want to miss this."

Longarm said slowly, "Might be, Mrs. Thompson, you don't have as great a seat as you think you do. Might be that the horse race is going to be run someplace else—someplace completely out of sight of here."

"Oh, I'm sure that at least I'll be able to hear the sound of the race, if not actually see it."

After a few more words, she took her empty coffee cup and went back into the kitchen and brought him a piece of peach pie. She said, "I've got work to do, Marshal. I'll leave you to finish your meal."

When he was through eating, he went upstairs to his room, got a bottle of whiskey and a glass, and then went down and knocked on Mr. Hawkins's door. A gruff, "Come in!" came from inside. Longarm opened the door and looked in. Hawkins was sitting at a small table in his shirtsleeves, wearing sleeve garters. He was playing solitaire.

Longarm said, "Who's winning?"

Hawkins looked up. "I would be, if I'd allow myself to cheat. Things have come to a sorry pass when a man won't even allow himself to cheat in a game of solitaire."

"Do you mind if we have that talk now?" said Longarm.

Hawkins ran his hand through his thinning hair. He said, "I was halfway hoping that we'd never get around to it. I was halfway hoping I had just dreamed that I had become . . . what's the word . . . an assistant deputy marshal?"

"Auxiliary deputy marshal."

"Well," said Hawkins, "I was hoping that the whole thing was a bad dream, and that it all wasn't going to take place. You might as well come in and sit down. I see you brought your supplies with you, so you must be going to make a stretch out of it."

Longarm walked in, kicking the door behind himself, and sat down in the chair facing Hawkins. He poured himself out a glass and then put the cork back in the bottle. He said, "I take it you don't drink out of preference."

Hawkins looked up. He said, "I don't drink because I can't drink. I like it too well. You get me started with one, and two weeks later, you'll find me in some town I don't even know how I got to, lying in bed with some woman I've never seen before, and without a penny in my pocket. You follow what I'm talking about?"

Longarm laughed. He said, "Oh, yeah, I understand that."

"So you just go ahead and guzzle all the firewater you want to. I'd just as soon stay in my right mind."

"It doesn't bother you if I drink in front of you?"

Hawkins said, "Hell, no. It just reinforces the idea that I'm doing the right thing. At least I know I'm sane. Of course, I'm not so sure about you, after you told me about that damned idea. Would you mind telling me what kind of saddle I'm supposed to lure Archie Barrett into town to see?"

Longarm took a sip of whiskey. "Well, now that you mention it, I have been giving that some thought, and I might have an idea on the subject."

Hawkins said, "Well, it's going to have to be one hell of a saddle. That's all I can tell you."

"You know, the president of Mexico got himself killed not too long ago. Now, what if your company just happened to have gotten a-hold of his number-one, main parade saddle. What do you think of that?"

"It'd be a damned miracle. That's what I think. Hell, a saddle like that . . ." He whistled. "A saddle like that would be worth plenty. Hell, I've heard that it's gold-mounted, made out of the finest leather. Yeah, something like that would definitely influence a man like Archie Barrett. But how come I don't take it to him?''

"Because your company has sent it down here special. There's two fellows that are guarding it, and it can't get out of their sight. They've got it in a wagon here in town and they're going on and the team's too tired to make it out to the Barrett ranch. You've got this one opportunity to show it to him. You tell him that you wired your headquarters and got them to come out of their way into Grit with that saddle. You ain't got much time, but it's his only chance to look at it.''

Hawkins was getting a gleam in his eye as if he actually had such a saddle for sale. "You know, a saddle like that would fetch right around two thousand five hundred dollars, maybe three thousand dollars.'' He whistled again. "My commission on that would run right around five, six hundred dollars. That's not a bad deal. You know, I can see where Archie Barrett would be interested in a saddle like that and he could afford it, priced at three thousand dollars. A man like that, the more he pays for something, the more he thinks it's worth. Yeah, yeah, that just might work. Maybe even three thousand five hundred dollars. What do you think about that?''

Longarm was watching in amazement as the leather goods drummer worked himself up. He said, "Why stop there? Why not make it a four thousand dollar saddle?''

Hawkins nodded vigorously. He said, "That's even better. Yeah, that's even better.'' He stopped and looked at Longarm. He said, "By the way, how did my company manage to come into possession of that saddle?''

Longarm said, "Why, that's easy. It was stolen out of the palace by some of them revolutionaries and one of them wound up in Del Rio and he sold it to one of your drummers that was working down there. Now y'all have got it to sell. It was brought up to the border and it fell into your hands. Now it can fall into Mr. Archie Barrett's hands. He'll be the envy of the territory. Jake Myers won't have anything like that.''

Hawkins said dryly, "Why don't you just leave the selling to me, Marshal? I believe I can come up with a talk that will work.''

"Excuse me, Mr. Hawkins. I didn't mean to get into your territory. I was just trying to help out.''

Hawkins sat there thinking. "I'm looking for holes in this proposition. Now, you do know that Mr. Archie Barrett is not going to ride into Grit by himself. He's going to have two or three men with him, and they won't be no second-rate gunslingers, either. He's got some first-class hands.''

Longarm said dryly, "Why don't you leave that to me, Mr. Hawkins. You do the selling, and I'll do the other part. That's my job.''

Hawkins gave him a stern look. He said, "You right sure you can handle it, Marshal? I'm going to be in the midst of that bunch coming in, and I'd just as soon not get killed until I have one last drunk. If I'm going to get killed, I might as well finish that bottle for you.''

Longarm shook his head slowly and clicked his tongue. He said, "Tsk, tsk, tsk, Mr. Hawkins. You don't want to break your resolve over a little thing like this. You'd feel silly if you got yourself all drunked up and then didn't get killed.''

Hawkins gave him a look. "I suppose you have a point, Marshal. But, say, are you certain that I am under obligation, that I've got to do this under the Constitution?''

Longarm gave him an eye. He said, "Mr. Hawkins, there are a few things I don't tease about. Pussy is one of them, good whiskey is another, and the law and my job are the other two. So I am dead serious when I tell you that you are a fully constituted member of the United States Marshal Service and subject to my orders. If you don't follow them, you can go to prison.''

Hawkins looked up at him. He said, ''That's a fine how do you do. A law-abiding citizen like me ends up like this.'' He began gathering up the cards. ''Well, the least you can do is play me some head-up poker. Maybe I can make a profit off that deal. Hell, two dollars a day! Why, that wouldn't even pay for my whiskey in other days and times.''

Longarm said as he reached into his pocket for his roll of money, ''I wouldn't count on it paying anything. Playing me poker doesn't generally improve a man's pocket. In fact, you might lose your two dollars a day for a long time to come.''

Hawkins began to shuffle the cards. He said, ''We'll just see about that, Marshal. Or do I call you boss?''

Longarm smiled. He said, ''Either one of them will do, Mr. Hawkins. Just shuffle them cards and give me a cut. And ante up a dollar while you got it.''

Chapter 7

The two men had finished playing poker and the cards had been put away. Now they were sitting, Longarm with a drink of whiskey and a cigarillo, and Mr. Hawkins with a pipe. Very little money had changed hands in the poker game, and the man had proven to be a rawhide-tough player, though Longarm claimed you couldn't tell anything about a man's skill by playing two-handed poker. He claimed it was about like trading horses blindfolded. He said, "Hell, it's all luck. You might as well turn them all faceup. Very few hands are going to come along where they are even enough to get some decent betting going."

It was growing late and Longarm was about to go back to his room. They had made their plans for the next day. Hawkins had groused a bit about delaying his departure for his next stop, but Longarm believed that he was secretly delighted to be a part of a law adventure.

Hawkins had wanted more details than Longarm had been able to supply about how they would operate the next day. Longarm simply said, "We leave here and along the road, I'm going to look for a likely spot. You're just going to go up to Archie Barrett's place. I'm going to wait for you. That's all it comes down to."

That had left Hawkins looking uneasy, but Longarm had reassured him by saying that he was a crack shot. He said, "Look at it this way, Mr. Hawkins. If it's you and Mr. Barrett and four riders, that's six people and I've got a one out of six chance of hitting you."

For a second, Hawkins stared at Longarm before he realized that his leg had been pulled. He said, "Aw shucks, Marshal. That kind of talk ain't funny, especially from a man wearing a badge on his chest."

Just before they were to leave, Longarm wanted the story about what happened to Mrs. Thompson's husband, Milton.

It brought a somber look to Hawkins's face. He said, "Maybe what happened to Milton Thompson is one of the main reasons I'm willing to go along with you on this foolishness. Milton was a good man. He came here and built this big house we're sitting in right now—fortunately for his wife or she wouldn't have a way to make her living—and he set about to make a community out of this place. He had some experience in banking and there were all these settlers coming in, most of them with little or no resources. They were a long way from the bank in Junction or the bank in Brady and certainly from the bank in Austin.

The man paused and looked at Longarm. "He proposed to set up a type of community bank. It wouldn't have been a regular bank, not in the same terms that you would think of one. It would be one that everybody put in a little money—twenty-five dollars if you had it, fifty dollars if you had it, or one hundred dollars if you could. And then, they'd make loans to whoever was the most needy. It was a good idea, Marshal, the kind of idea that would have worked and the kind of idea that would have saved many of these settlers that were close to going under. Well, naturally, the Barretts and the Myerses didn't like it at all. Not only that, he was going to put up a feed and grocery cooperative, staples, work clothes and such so that these settlers could kind of own that and be able to buy whatever they needed at the cheapest possible price instead of being held up by some of these townspeople here who are scared to death of the Barretts and the Myerses.''

Hawkins paused again for a moment. ''See, at first, Jake Myers and the Barretts were content to just try and starve them out, but Milton Thompson got in the way of that. They rocked on like that for maybe a year or so until one of them, maybe both of them, got impatient. There was a string of riders came blazing through here at noon one day just as Milton Thompson was walking across the street from the little building he called a bank to take his noon meal with his wife. They shot him down in the street. They put enough holes in him that he looked like a colander right in front of his wife and in full view of half of the town. The townspeople knew who those riders and gunmen were. I wasn't here at the time, but I arrived a week later. It was a sad sight. So, that's the story of Milton Thompson.''

Longarm adjusted his hat. The story made him feel bad. He said, ''And Mrs. Thompson was willing to try and hang on?''

Hawkins nodded. He said, ''Yes, she even tried to run the bank for awhile. In fact,'' and he smiled at this, ''it was one of those storefront kind of places. The last one on the end on the east side. She put up a sign on the front that said Kill Me If You Dare. She's a pistol. She's got a lot of bottom to her, a lot of grit.''

Longarm said, "I'm afraid she's had just about enough, though."

Hawkins shrugged. "Yes, and I don't blame her. She couldn't make the bank go. It was a narrow thing as it was, a near thing. It didn't have one chance in a hundred, anyway, and without Milton Thompson to drive it, it had no chance at all. Everybody came in and got what little money they had in it and that pretty well blew it up. Somebody else bought the feed store. Sims works over at the mercantile. I think Myers owns it; I'm not sure. You're looking at a ghost town that is in the midst of happening. All these settlers will soon be gone and all this land will end up being divided as they intended from the very first between the Myerses and the Barretts. That is, unless you think you can stop it. I don't think you can, not without a troop of calvary."

Longarm shook his head slowly. He said, "Mr. Hawkins, we just don't have that many troops of calvary that we can bring in every time there's a dispute over government land. If we did, we'd have to draft every man, woman, and child in the United States and put them in a blue uniform and put them on permanent duty down here in the Southwest. This damned stuff is so common, it makes the wax run out of your ears. No sir. They gave me this job to do and as much as I dislike it, and as dull a job as it is, I am going to get it done. I am sorry to hear about Mr. Thompson. That's sad when a man is trying to help his neighbors and that's the kind of end he gets. And it's sad the fact of the business about his wife. She seems like a wonderful woman. It's a damned shame that she has to lose what she had in such a hard fashion."

Hawkins gave Longarm a bemused look. The lank man said, "She's a handsome woman, Mrs. Thompson is. I don't think she needs to be a widow long. Do you, Marshal?"

Longarm frowned. He said, "I'm not studying on affairs

that don't concern me right now, Mr. Hawkins. What we've got to do is get our minds set for tomorrow. What you've got to do is start believing that you've got the president of Mexico's saddle here, and that you're going to give Mr. Archie Barrett a chance to buy it for four thousand dollars.''

George Hawkins smiled sardonically. He said, ''Yeah, I never thought I'd see the day that I would have such a prize to sell. I'm amazed at my luck, myself. I can't tell you, Marshal, how anxious I am to hightail it out there right in the middle of that beehive and tell Archie Barrett such a lie. You know, of course, I'm not going to be able to ever come back to this part of the country again.''

''I've been waiting for you to bring that up,'' Longarm said. ''You don't have to worry about that, Mr. Hawkins. The way I'm going to handle this affair, Barrett will never know that you ever had anything to do with it. You don't have to worry. You might hear a bullet sing over your head, but other than that, you just do what you get told to do when you get told to do it, and you won't have to worry.''

Hawkins shook his head slowly from side to side. He said, ''Well, Marshal. I don't know why, but for some reason, I trust you. Of course, as it works out, I ain't got no choice. If I don't do what you tell me, you'll put me in prison. That's about the size of it, isn't it?''

Longarm stood up and picked up his whiskey and his glass. He said, ''Yeah, and we'd better get to bed. I want to get started on this little project pretty early, so I reckon I'll see you at breakfast.''

Hawkins stood up, too. He said, ''I doubt I'll be able to swallow a mouthful of food, I'm that nervous.''

Longarm looked at him and laughed. He said, ''Mr. Hawkins, you're a liar. You're not a damned bit nervous. In fact, I've got the sneaking suspicion that you're enjoying this.''

Hawkins tried to look shocked, but he didn't quite bring

it off. He said, "Why, the very idea, Marshal! This is not my kind of work. This is dangerous. As far as I know, the only dangerous thing I ever did was sell a man a pair of boots that were a half size too small."

Longarm laughed and let himself out of the room. He walked back down to his own and commenced getting ready for bed.

They were on their way by a little after eight o'clock. George Hawkins was riding his mare, and Longarm was atop his roan gelding. Very few people were on the streets to see them as they departed. As they crossed the prairie at a slow lope, Hawkins said, "I hope you understand, Marshal, that you're dealing with a man that ain't used to gunfire and weapons and those sort of things."

Longarm turned slightly in his saddle to give Hawkins a look. He said, "Mr. Hawkins, you might think you can conceal it from everybody else, but you don't conceal it from me. You wear that frock coat because inside it, you carry a long-barrel, .38 caliber, six-shot revolver. Now, anybody that carries a long-barrel—and it appeared to be about a nine-inch barrel—is planning on making some long-distance revolver shots. That means he knows what he's doing. He's not planning on getting up next to somebody and shooting them in the belly. So, I wish you wouldn't start the morning off by lying to me. You have no idea what that does to my confidence in you."

Hawkins chuckled slightly. He said, "Why, Marshal, I never thought you'd take notice of such a thing. I've got a clever little pocket built into my coat where that nice little gun just fits. You ain't supposed to see that."

"Yeah, I'm supposed to see it, Mr. Hawkins. The reason I'm supposed to see it is why I'm still alive today. What I don't know, is why you carry it."

97

Hawkins said, "Well, from time to time, I do a little cash business, and I have discovered that there are people in this world who will try to take advantage of you. Even to the point of attempting to relieve you of your cash. Now, my company takes a dim view of that, and so do I."

Longarm said, "I can understand that. Just don't tell me anymore that you're not a man used to weapons and guns and other such frightening instruments."

The morning was cool, and they rode toward the southwest. Longarm was looking for a specific situation. He wanted a place of ambush. He wanted a place to hide himself and his horse where he could still have a clear view of any party that would be oncoming, headed toward town. According to Hawkins, it was about six miles to the Barretts' place, perhaps less. Longarm would have liked to take them no more than two or three miles from town. The closer they got to the ranch, the less he was going to like it. They had been riding for maybe twenty-five minutes when he spied a grove of cottonwood trees just ahead. Cottonwood trees generally grew near water, so there was a good chance that a stream or a gully that collected water was nearby. Within five minutes, they had come up to the little clump of trees. The cottonwoods were of good size, being at least two feet in diameter, and there were about ten or twelve of them. A little dry bed lay to the south of the trees that probably filled up in flood times and in times of heavy rains.

Longarm brought them to a stop. He said, "I believe this may just do it, Mr. Hawkins. How far would you say we are from the Barretts' headquarters?"

Hawkins turned in his saddle, looked back, and then looked forward. He said, "I'd reckon that we're close to halfway. It's about three miles back to town, maybe not quite that." He pulled his watch out of his pocket and consulted the time. "We've been gone close to thirty minutes. Yeah, it's about three miles back. We're near enough to the midway point that I wouldn't argue the difference with you."

Longarm dismounted and dropped the reins of his horse to the ground. He said, "All right, Mr. Hawkins. Now it's up to you. You've got to go in there and sell that man on the idea of a saddle. You've got to bring him back by these trees. This is where I'm going to be."

A flicker of doubt crossed the skinny man's face. "I hope you understand, Marshal, that he ain't going to be alone. He'll have four or five riders with him, at least."

Longarm said, "I'm prepared for that. Just keep your head down. You ain't going to get shot unless you shoot yourself."

Hawkins still looked worried. "Could be they'll think I had something to do with this. One of them just might decide to plug me."

Longarm said with no attempt at bragging, "Your safety is going to be my first concern. If I see anybody throw down on you, that'll be the man I shoot. I give you my word, you'll come to no harm."

Hawkins stared down at him from atop his mare. He said, "Well, Marshal, I'll give you this. You're a man who believes in himself. I just wish I could believe the same amount."

"You had better go along now. Just believe in your mind that you've got that assassinated president's saddle back there and it's a wonder and it's the best thing you've ever sold. You hate to let go of it, but you'll be proud to see it in the hands of such a fine fellow as Archie Barrett."

Hawkins gave him a sour look. "Now you are asking me to lie a little more than I can handle. My boat won't float but just so many lies, and you're about to overload me."

Longarm smiled. He reached over his horse and pulled his .44 caliber, lever-action Winchester rifle out of the boot. He said, "Go on along, now, and bring me back a surprise."

Hawkins put the spurs to his mare and said over his shoulder, "Yeah, that's just what I wanted at my age. A nice surprise."

Longarm watched him lope away, riding with the easy slouch and seat of an accomplished horseman. He reckoned that Hawkins could tell many a tale about his life in front of the campfire, especially if you ever got another drink in him. But he had to admire the man. There weren't all that many that would admit when something had the best of them and they had to put it down or lose everything. Hawkins had been smart enough not to crow about it. Still, Longarm reckoned just from the way the man carried himself and the look in his eye that George Hawkins had lit more than one bonfire in his life and had outrun more than one stampede.

After Hawkins had gone over a rise and dipped partially out of sight, Longarm led his mount into the grove of cottonwoods. For himself, there was plenty of cover. He figured he was in for a long wait. His only worry was that Hawkins would arrive too late in the morning and Barrett wouldn't want to make the trip into town until after the noon meal. That would be a long wait out in the prairie, and he didn't relish that. Still, it was pretty country to look at, with the good grass and the mesquite trees and here and there, oak, cottonwood, and willows. Sometimes a line of willows would run right across a piece of flat prairie. That was a sure indicator there was underground water near the surface. It was a land well blessed with all the natural resources that a man needed to make a good living. It was a shame it had been deviled by two greedy sons of bitches.

Of course, there were more than just two. Archie Barrett and Jake Myers weren't the only ones. They had the full help and cooperation of their families and friends. Everybody wanted to feed at the trough. Longarm wondered if the day wouldn't come, through natural selection, that they would kill each other off. Of course, that would take a spell, and the people who were really suffering would be long gone by then.

Longarm hunkered down beside a cottonwood and took out a cigarillo and lit it. It was safe enough, this early in time, for him to be smoking. He also had a bottle of whiskey in his saddlebags along with his extra revolver. He didn't feel like a drink, however. Mrs. Thompson had loaded them up with a good breakfast of scrambled eggs and fried potatoes. Longarm had eaten until he thought he'd pop. She was an outstanding woman. Steadfast, a good cook, a good homemaker, a good mother, and pretty damned good looking in the bargain. He doubted that she would stay on the market very long once she made up her mind to take off her widow's weeds. Longarm didn't think that she could feel easy in her mind so long as her husband's killers still ran rampant over the land that he had tried to improve.

Time passed, and Longarm grew restless. He got out his watch a half dozen times. It came nine thirty, it came nine forty, and then nine forty-five. Gradually, it became ten o'clock and he was starting to seriously worry that if Hawkins was able to talk Archie Barrett into coming into Grit to look at the saddle, that the two men would be waiting until after lunch. He didn't know if he would have the patience to stay still that long. There was so much riding on this throw of the dice that he was anxious to get it over with. He calculated in his own mind that if Hawkins would be turned down, he would start back as soon as he saw that it was hopeless. Longarm calculated that would put him coming back by the cottonwoods around ten thirty, ten forty at the outside. So, if he hadn't seen Hawkins by that time, he thought he could be fairly certain that Archie Barrett had taken the bait.

All he could do was wait. He smoked about a half dozen cigarillos and finally had taken a drink of the whiskey when it came to be ten twenty. For the twelfth time, he closed his watch and put it back in his pocket. He worked the lever of his rifle, looking at the chamber, making sure that a shell was there. He pulled the hammer back to half cock and then to full cock and then he gently let it back down.

Finally, he turned his back to the direction in which either Mr. Hawkins or the whole party would be coming. He wouldn't look for another ten minutes. No, he wouldn't look for fifteen minutes. He settled back, resting his head against the trunk of the tree, looking up at the canopy of sky above the leafy tops of the cottonwoods.

Five minutes passed. He heard his horse make a little nickering sound. It wasn't much, but it was something. He eased up into a squatting position and looked toward his animal. The horse had his ears pricked up and was staring in the direction George Hawkins had ridden off.

Longarm stood up and peeked slowly around the trunk of the tree he had been resting against. In the distance, perhaps two miles off, he could see several black dots coming his way.

He watched them steadily as they went down a depression and then came up another rise. They were much closer now, and he could tell they were moving at a fairly good clip, something short of a gallop but faster than a slow lope. He doubted that Archie Barrett or any of his men cared much about the way they used horses.

Now, they were getting close. He could identify Hawkins. He was the second rider in from Longarm's right. There were three others besides George Hawkins. He took the man to Hawkins's immediate right to be Archie Barrett because of the way he was dressed. Hawkins was wearing his usual broadcloth frock coat and the man to his right was dressed the same way. The two outriders were wearing wide-brimmed hats and chaps and shirts with kerchiefs around their necks. He reckoned them to be the guards that he thought Archie Barrett went everywhere with. He was surprised there were only two.

Now they were really close, only a hundred yards away. Longarm moved stealthfully to the tree on the outside of the little clump. His plan was to step out and stop the party. He could see that Hawkins was managing to guide them as close to the cottonwood clump as he could. They had slowed now to a trot as they approached the gully that ran right in front of the cottonwoods. In another second, they would be within voice range. The whole point was to get Archie Barrett, but Longarm's main intent was to make sure nothing happened to Mr. Hawkins. His finger was going to be very steady on the trigger and his instincts were going to be very quick to react.

When the horsemen were fifteen or twenty yards away, Longarm stepped out from behind the tree, his rifle cocked and at the ready. His sudden appearance caused them to check their horses. Longarm called out in a loud voice, "Halt! Stop! This is the law!"

They came to a halt some fifteen yards away. Longarm could tell that they were confused. He recognized the outside rider to his right. It was the man with the torn ear, and he knew almost in the same instant they had pulled their horses up that the man was going to go for his gun. He knew that the man was going to try something different, but Longarm was ready. He saw the man begin to slip sideways out of the saddle, and he shot the hired hand before he could get half-way off his horse. The bullet hit the man in the upper right part of his chest and drove him the rest of the way to the ground. He knew the man had been planning on dropping off the left side of his horse and then making a shot from under the animal.

Longarm had no time to dwell on that. Already, with the sound of his rifle still ringing in his ears, he was swinging on the gunman to his immediate left. The man had drawn his revolver and was in the act of cocking it when Longarm shot him just below the throat. The rider went backwards, one boot hanging up in his stirrup so that as he fell off, he hit the ground with his legs still in the air. His horse bolted forward and dragged him a few yards until his foot came out of the boot, and then he lay on his back on the prairie.

Hawkins, acting as surprised as if it were all news to him, had thrown both of his hands in the air and yelled, "Don't shoot! Don't shoot!"

The ranch boss had made no move for a gun. Instead, Archie Barrett had kept both hands on the horn of his saddle. He sat there, stolid, not moving, in a black suit and vest and a black, narrow-brimmed derby. He said, "What is this? Robbery? What are you after?"

Longarm walked closer to the man, his rifle at the ready. He said, "Are you Archie Barrett?"

The man, who was of large girth and had a small mustache said, "That's my name. What's it to you?"

Longarm guessed him to be in his mid-thirties. He was dark-haired but had a surprisingly light complexion for one who must have lived some of his life outdoors. Longarm said, "My name is Custis Long. I am a United States deputy marshal. You're under arrest."

Barrett stared at him. He said, "You've got no call to arrest me. I'm a private citizen on private business. You have killed two of my men. You, sir, will pay for this."

Longarm said, "Who's this other man?" He nodded his head at Hawkins.

Barrett said, "If you want to know so bad, ask him yourself. It's none of my affair. I'm going back to my ranch."

Longarm pulled the hammer back on his Winchester. He said, "You make one move to turn your horse in the wrong direction, Mr. Barrett, and I can guarantee that it'll be the last move you ever make."

Barrett stared at him defiantly. He said, "You wouldn't dare. I'm an important man, a money man, a man with friends in high places."

Longarm said evenly, "You turn that horse the wrong way, and you're going to be a man with friends in low places. Six feet low. As far as I'm concerned, if you turn your back on me, you'll be an escaping prisoner, and I won't have the slightest hesitation about shooting you down. Do I make myself clear?"

For answer, Barrett stared sullenly back at him. He said, "You have killed two of my men in cold blood. I'll see you hang for that."

Longarm nodded his head slightly, first to the left and then to the right to where the men lay on the ground. He said, "If you'll take notice, and I call on this other gentleman to take notice, both of those men have drawn pistols near them. They were both killed in self-defense and in the line of duty, just as you are now under arrest in the line of duty, Mr. Barrett."

Barrett said, "What are your grounds for arresting me?"

"I'm getting damned tired of talking to you, Barrett. Now, you see those two horses that are loose? They're starting to step on their reins. You get off your horse and go over there and tie their reins back behind the saddle horns. Then give them a lick on the hip and send them back to your ranch. I expect they'll go back to the ranch, unless they're stolen."

Barrett didn't move. "I'm not catching up any horses."

Longarm took several deliberate steps toward the black figure on the horse. He stood just beside the man who had his hands held so delicately on the saddle horn. He said, "Barrett, I'll warn you one more time. Get off your horse and rig those reins on those two loose ponies before they tear their mouths out stepping on their reins."

Barrett looked down at him contemptuously. He said, "Go to hell."

With a swift, sudden movement, Longarm reversed the Winchester in his hands and drove the butt stock of it into Barrett's ample stomach. The man gasped as the air went out of him, and his face contorted with pain. He sagged sideways in the saddle. Longarm drew the Winchester back to give him another blow. He said, "You want some more?"

Barrett put up a weak hand. He said in a strangled voice, "Hold it, hold it. I'm hurt."

"You're fixing to be hurt a lot worse."

Just then, Hawkins said, "Marshal, how about letting me? I'm used to handling livestock, a good deal more than Mr. Barrett here. This poor man has been through a hard and trying day."

"And just who might you be, sir?" Longarm said. He turned to face George Hawkins and gave him a wink.

Hawkins said, "I'm just a leather peddler. I'd been out making a call on Mr. Barrett to show him a saddle. We were just peacefully going down to look at that saddle."

Longarm said, "Then, I reckon you'll be coming along with us. All right, get off your horse and tie the reins back on those two ponies and turn them back toward home."

Hawkins slid gracefully out of his saddle and then caught up the first of the horses of the two dead men and quickly tied its reins behind the saddle horn so that they wouldn't be interfered with. He caught up the other one and did the same with it. After that, he led both horses in the direction of Barrett's ranch and gave them a hoot and holler and a slap on the rump and sent them on their way.

By the time he had finished, some of the color had come back to Barrett's face, though he was still leaning over in his saddle, holding his middle. Longarm said, "Have I got to tell you something twice again, Barrett?"

Archie Barrett wouldn't look up nor would he speak.

Longarm said, "I asked you a question, and you better damned well answer it, or you're going to get some more where you don't want it. Do I have to tell you something twice again?"

In a sullen voice, Barrett said, "No, I suppose not, Marshal. If you really are a marshal."

"You'll find out soon enough how much of a marshal I am." Longarm motioned at Hawkins. He said, "Y'all start on ahead. Ride to the east. I don't want you getting within a mile of town. I'll be right behind you. Don't think you can outrun me, because I'm riding a good horse."

Hawkins said, "Marshal, I'd never think of doing any such of a thing. Me and Mr. Barrett, we are law-abiding citizens. I don't know what you could want with us, anyway."

Longarm, trying to keep a straight face, said, "Well, right now, I don't want you, but if you keep on talking as smart as you have been, it may well be that I can find a jail cell for you, too."

Longarm went into the cottonwood grove, untied his horse, and mounted it. He slid the rifle home in the boot and set out in pursuit of Barrett and Hawkins, who were a couple of hundred yards ahead. He closed within ten yards and then rode silently behind them. He knew that Hawkins understood that they were going to Tom Hunter's place, but from time to time, he would direct Barrett to veer more to the northeast so that it would not seem that George Hawkins knew their destination.

He said on one occasion, "I don't think you want to be seen from town, Mr. Barrett, so let's stay well south of it. I don't think you've got too many friends there right now."

Barrett looked over his shoulder. "I'd reckon I've got more friends in there than you do. I've heard about your policy of not allowing anyone to trade there if they worked for me or my brothers or Jake Myers. That's not any way to get on the good side of anyone, Marshal. If a marshal's really what you are."

Longarm said, "I haven't seen too much evidence, Barrett, that you've been on the good side of anybody. You just keep that horse pointed in the direction that I'm telling you, and you and I will get along just fine."

"I demand to know where you're taking me."

Longarm said, "You can demand all you want to, but it's not going to do you any good. I'm going to take you someplace where you and I can have a nice quiet talk about what's been going on around here for the past two or three years. A place where you and I can have a talk about a lot of dead bodies and a lot of burned-out cabins and a lot of stolen and killed cattle."

Barrett said without turning his head, "I don't know nothing about no such thing, Marshal Long."

"So, you know my name." Longarm suddenly laughed. "Word must have gotten back around to you."

The back of Archie Barrett's neck went red. He said, "Word gets around, Marshal. Word gets around. You've done everything you could to kick up a ruckus since you got here. My only regret is that I didn't have you attended to before now."

"Well, the fact is, Barrett, you did try. I don't know what that old boy's name is with half an ear, but you sent him in the other day to have a go with me. It didn't work, but that was your plan. Was he your top gunhand, Barrett? I would reckon he was. What was his name, by the way?"

"That wouldn't be any of your business."

"Oh, I think I'll find out soon enough."

"What kind of lawman are you that would leave two men laying dead out on the prairie?"

Longarm said, "I'm not going to do a damned thing, Barrett. If those two horses belong to your headquarters, they'll show up there, and then I would guess that some of your men will go looking for them. I reckon they'll find the bodies. Or don't those horses belong to your headquarters? Are they some of the gunhands' that you brought in here that their horses ain't learned where home is yet? I wouldn't be surprised if that was the case. How many hired hands you got that actually punch cattle on your place?"

Hawkins said in a grieved voice, "Marshal, don't you think you're being awfully hard on Mr. Barrett? He's been a good customer of mine for a number of years, and I hate to hear you vilify a man of such character."

Longarm said, "Listen, leather drummer. You'd better just sit that horse and keep your mouth shut, or I'm liable to shoot that so-called hat off your head. What do you call that thing, anyway?"

"It's a proper fedora, Marshal."

"Well, it's a damned silly-looking thing. A hat is supposed to have enough brim to shade your face or catch the rainwater. You and Barrett are both wearing hats that ain't good for nothing that I could see. Now, move it on up a little bit. That old nag you're riding, can't she do much more than shuffle along?"

Even though George Hawkins must have known he was kidding, he was still stung enough to turn in the saddle and give Longarm a look. He said, "Why? Would you care to race?"

Longarm smiled gleefully. He said, "I wouldn't mind, but first I'd have to handcuff you to Mr. Barrett. You reckon you could beat me dragging him?"

In the distance, he could see just the tops of the town buildings as they rounded to the south and turned up toward the northeast. They were about two miles from Tom Hunter's cabin. It was closing on twelve o'clock. He hoped ferverantly that Tom had been able to get the Goodmans to come and join him. His whole plan depended on being able to keep his prisoner secluded and guarded and protected.

As they bypassed the town, Hawkins said in a plaintive voice, "Marshal, you ain't said nothing about me being under arrest, and I've got business in town. Would it be all right with you if I just split off here and rode on in?"

Not knowing how his plan might work or if it would work or what further use the man might be, it was important to Longarm and to George Hawkins himself that Archie Barrett continue to think that he had just been an innocent bystander caught up in the net that Longarm had cast. He assumed and hoped that Barrett would not connect his trip into town with Hawkins with Longarm's interception.

Longarm said, "Now, look here, mister leather fellow, I don't know who you are or what your business is, but for the time being, I reckon you'll just come along with us. So far as I'm concerned, the first thing you might do is scramble back to the Barrett ranch and spread the word. Right now, I don't want that happening. So you just might as well settle down and make yourself at home."

Barrett said, again in a sullen voice, "Where the hell are you taking me? And by what authority are you taking me?"

Longarm said, "Barrett, if you don't shut up, I'm going to see if I can't shoot one of your ears off like that one gunslinger of yours laying back there on the ground. Maybe you'll come to the same end as him. You keep fucking around with me, and I can guarantee you will. Just keep your horse pointed in the direction it's going and keep your mouth shut."

Within another half hour, Tom Hunter's place came into view from a long distance off. It was set upon a little crown of land with its good stone house and its neat outbuildings and corrals. As they neared, Longarm could see that there were some cattle, more than just the ten that Hunter claimed to have, being close herded near the house. It was his guess that it meant that the Goodmans had arrived. That was a relief.

Barrett suddenly turned in his saddle and said, "That's Tom Hunter's place up there. We're not going anywhere near there, are we?"

Longarm said, "Oh, Tom Hunter. You know him, do you?"

"What the hell business is it of yours whether I know him? Of course I know him. I know just about everyone around here."

"And have stolen cattle off of damned near everybody around here, I understand. I guess the only reason you haven't burned out Tom Hunter is that his house is made out of rock and he's a pretty good hand with a rifle. I hear he's shorted you a few hired hands. Is that right?"

"Go to hell."

"Not as fast as you, neighbor. Now, get that horse to moving."

They rode steadily forward until they started up the rise to Hunter's house. Fifty yards away, Longarm saw Tom Hunter step through the front door, a rifle in his hands. They rode up and the rancher came forward, nodding his head.

Hunter said, "Howdy Marshal." He glanced over at Barrett. "I see you brought our visitor."

Longarm looked at Barrett and saw that the man looked alarmed. Barrett said, "What the hell does he mean, his visitor? You're not keeping me here. I am not staying in this man's house. Marshal, you cannot do this."

Longarm swung his leg over his saddle and dismounted. He said, "Get down, Barrett. You can rest your legs for a while, and you can also rest that mouth of yours."

"I'm not getting off this horse."

Longarm walked around the flank of his own horse and approached Barrett with his rifle reversed and the butt end facing the chunky man. He said, "Get down or get knocked off that horse. Take your choice. I'll give you about one second to decide."

Barrett began to cuss, but he also swung his leg over and dismounted with a grunt. He was heftier than Longarm had thought at first. It was clear that he hadn't done much hard work in some time.

Tom Hunter said, "I've got a room all ready for him."

"Did Mr. Goodman and his boy get here?" Longarm said.

"Yeah, they're getting their stock settled."

Barrett swung around to face both of them. He said, "What the hell is going on? What are you playing at? If you are trying something that you will be sorry for, I promise you I will make you sorry for it. You are not going to detain me here."

Longarm said, "Walk on into the house, Mr. Barrett, or else we'll carry you in. It makes no difference to me, one way or the other."

With Tom Hunter and Hawkins following, Longarm shoved Archie Barrett into the front room of the cabin. It was dim and cool. Longarm said over his shoulder to Hunter, "Which way?"

"Straight ahead. There's a small room that my wife used to use for sewing and whatnot. It's bare now. She took what furniture and other little items she could with her. Got a good stout door on it and the windows are mighty small. I think it would take a hell of a big window to get his fat butt out."

Longarm shoved Barrett ahead of him and to the right and

112

through a door that opened into a room that was about ten feet by ten feet. There was a window in each of the two outside walls, but they were up high and as Tom had said, they were small. There was a chair and a table in the room and a wash basin and a pitcher of water. There was nothing else.

Longarm looked around and said, "Fine. This ought to do it." He backed out and pulled the heavy wooden door shut behind him and then turned the key in the lock. On the other side, he heard a sudden yell and a stream of curses.

He turned around and smiled at Tom Hunter and at Hawkins. He said, "Now, I think we'll let him cool out for a while and let him meditate on his sins."

Tom Hunter said, "How long do you reckon?"

"Oh, all night for certain, and that with no supper."

"Do you reckon we ought to put a bucket in there for him?"

"There's a pitcher, ain't there? And a wash bowl?"

"Yeah, but that's for him to drink and wash his face."

Longarm shrugged. "Hell, he can take his choice."

The men sat talking for a few minutes. Tom Hunter started frying up some bacon and beans. In a little while, the two Goodmans came in. If Longarm hadn't been told different, he would have thought they were brothers rather than father and son. They were both on the smallish side. Longarm guessed they each weighed somewhere between one hundred and forty and one hundred and fifty pounds. They were square built with square shoulders and square hands and thick necks and they both looked very solid and very capable. The father, Robert, was not quite as blond as his son, but his eyes were equally blue. The son, Rufus, had a little thinner face, but Longarm reckoned it would square up to match his father's when a few years had passed.

While the bacon was frying, they sat around the big table

113

and discussed the matter at hand. As best as he could, Longarm explained his plan. Tom Hunter was the most enthusiastic. The Goodmans seemed to have a number of doubts. Robert Goodman said, "I don't see how you're going to be able to force him to keep his word. That's what I don't see."

Longarm said, "You leave that part to me. That's law work. And by the way, speaking of law work, Mr. Hawkins here is already sworn in as an auxiliary deputy marshal. Y'all three are now sworn in as auxiliary deputy marshals."

Rufus, the son, said, "Ain't we supposed to hold up our hands or something?"

Longarm gave him a dry look. He said, "Son, it ain't the ceremony that counts. But do understand this: you are now duly constituted law officers, and you've got to act within the law, whatever you do. I'm responsible for you, so I'm going to make damned sure that you don't misuse it. But, being within the law, whatever you do will be legal."

Rufus said, jerking his head toward the room where Archie Barrett was still yelling at the top of his voice, "Is what you're doing with that fellow in there inside the law?"

Longarm said, "Son, whatever I do is within the law. That don't apply to all of y'all, but it applies to me."

Mr. Hawkins said, "You're pretty easy with that law. You kind of make it up as you go along?"

"Why, Mr. Hawkins, how can you make such a statement?"

Hawkins shook his head. "Because you have shanghaied me. I'm not even supposed to be here, and now you're laying out plans that are going to keep me here four or five more days. What am I supposed to tell my company? That I've quit them and gone into law work?"

Longarm said, "I'll give you a note for your boss. It'll make it all right."

But it was Robert Goodman who said what Longarm thought needed to be said: "Well, Marshal, I don't have any idea if this plan of yours will work, either, but I do know there ain't many ways that these folks can be got at, and your way sounds as good as any I can think of if you give me ten years to think of it. What's important to me and to Rufus and to Tom is that somebody from the outside is trying to help us. The way it was before is that we've been sitting down here being picked off one by one. They've took the weak ones and now they are down to just us. We haven't succumbed so easy, but it would be just a matter of time before they wiped us out. The only reason they haven't just massacred the bunch of us is that I figure that it would have caused so much of a ruckus that maybe even somebody in the state capital would have cared. I'm with you, me and Rufus, all the way, and I appreciate what you're doing."

Longarm said, "Thank you, Mr. Goodman. We'll just roll the dice and see what happens."

Tom Hunter said, "One thing's for certain: it can't be no worse than what it was. I was about a week from up and leaving."

Robert Goodman added, "I doubt if we would have lasted the week. We're down to eight cows. We couldn't have gone on much longer."

Tom Hunter got up to turn the bacon over and to stir the beans. Hawkins said, cocking an ear toward the room they had Archie Barrett in, "He is kicking up a ruckus, ain't he?"

Rufus said, "Marshal Long, you just plan to starve him down? Just hold him down until he comes to his senses?"

Longarm said, "That's the only way I can do it, son. I don't know of any other way."

The boy said with a grim look, "How about you just turn me loose in there and lock the door behind me? I reckon I

115

can get him to agree to just about anything, and it'll take a hell of a lot less time.''

Longarm laughed. He said, "Yeah, we could take some skin off him, but not right off the bat. Let's do it this way for a while and see how it looks. I have a feeling he won't be too hard a nut to crack. He looks a might on the soft side to me.''

Hawkins nodded his head on his scrawny neck. "Archie Barrett might have been a pretty hard man at one time in his life, but that's long since past. He couldn't drink black coffee now if there was a prize for it. He's got to have cream for his coffee and butter for his bread. Hell, I bet he can't even eat corn bread. He eats nothing but light bread now. No, he's soft, Marshal. He's soft, but how willing he is to give in to the kind of demands you're going to put on him, I don't know.''

"We'll see," Longarm said.

From the small kitchen, Tom Hunter said, "You boys better get in here and get you a plate. What there is, is ready. You may not want it, but it's all we've got.''

While they ate, Hawkins said to Longarm, "You know, Marshal, I don't know if it's occurred to you or not, but you ain't even told Archie Barrett what you want of him. You reckon he might be willing by now?''

Longarm had to wait a moment while he swallowed a mouthful of very dry corn bread. He shot Tom Hunter a look as if to accuse him of being a dangerous man in the kitchen. He said to Hawkins, "No, I don't see any point of burdening the man's mind any more than need be. Right now, he's in that room and he's imagining worse things than I could ever tell him. Best thing, I reckon, that you can do with him is to let him sit and stew for a while. If you ever get in a gunfight with a fellow, Mr. Hawkins, make some excuse to

116

put it off for an hour. You'd be surprised at how shaky that other fellow's hand will get in an hour.''

Hawkins gave him a sardonic look. "What about your own hand?''

"Mine shakes all the time," Longarm said. "It don't make a difference to me.''

Young Rufus Goodman said, "Marshal, you know they're going to come looking for him, don't you?''

Longarm nodded. "I would reckon, but I don't think this is the first place they'll come. It'll take them some time to even get an idea that he's missing. I've also got an idea that he's got two brothers that might not much care. He's been the big cheese over them for quite some time, as I understand it. They might not want him found.''

"What do we do if they come looking here?'' said the older Goodman.

Longarm glanced at the man. "I was given to understand that you and your boy are pretty fair hands with a rifle. This cabin is made out of rock and we've got good, clear land all around us and we'll be shooting down. I'd say the odds are all on our side. If we can't stand off fifty men here, the five of us, something's wrong.''

"What about ammo?''

Longarm said, "I'm going into town in the morning to get some.'' He glanced over at Tom Hunter. "I'm also going to get a couple big sacks of grub that nobody can ruin.''

Tom Hunter said, "Listen, Marshal, if you'd like to take over the cooking, you're more than welcome. I've lost ten pounds since I've been cooking for myself. I've never been so tired of anything in my life as I am of bacon and beans, but those are the only things I know how to cook, short of slaughtering a cow and cutting off one steak.''

Rufus Goodman said, "Marshal, how long do you think this is going to take before he breaks?"

Longarm looked at him. He said, "Son, if I knew that, I'd be damned near as smart as a twenty-year-old."

Chapter 8

Longarm had Barrett brought out of his room the next morning about eleven o'clock. He had created a ruckus far into the previous night and then had fallen silent, only to begin again, pounding on the walls and yelling some time around daybreak. Finally, after a couple of hours, he had grown quiet again. Longarm had figured he was nearing the point of exhaustion.

He sent Tom Hunter and Robert Goodman to bring Barrett out. Longarm sat at the big dining table near the kitchen, faced in such a way that he would be the first sight that Barrett would see. He had sent Hawkins and the younger Goodman outside so Barrett would not know the strength of their numbers.

Barrett came out looking haggard and disheveled, but he was still angry. The minute he saw Longarm, he began to swell up and shout, "Damn it, you cur! What do you mean locking me in a room like that? You son of a bitch, I'll have you killed, marshal or not."

Longarm let him rattle on, shrieking and shouting until he finally quieted down. Then he nodded for Goodman and Hunter to bring the rancher over to the table where he had laid out a pen, a pot of ink, and a piece of paper. He said, "Set him in that chair."

There was a heavy smell of bacon in the cabin along with the smell of flapjacks. Longarm had sent young Rufus Goodman into town early that morning to buy a supply of .44 shells and some flour and some canned goods as well as a smoked ham. He could see Barrett sniffing the air. He knew a man that was used to eating as regularly as Barrett would be dying by now.

Barrett said, "You sons of bitches plan on starving me to death? I want something to eat and I want it right now."

Longarm said calmly, "Mr. Barrett, you can have something to eat and you can have much better treatment. All you have to do is write a letter for me."

Barrett looked at Longarm, his lip curling. He said, "You go to hell, you son of a bitch. I ain't writing nothing for you. What kind of a letter do you want me to write, anyway?"

Longarm said, "I want you to write a letter to Jake Myers asking him to meet you."

Barrett furrowed his brow. He said, "Why would I want to do a damfool thing like that? I don't want to see Jake Myers."

"No, but I do."

"Then, hell, write him yourself or go see him. I doubt you'd get out of there alive."

Longarm smiled. "Now, you're getting the general idea. No, I think I need you to write the letter. Now, here's the pen. Take it up, and I'll tell you what to write. When you're finished, you can have something to eat."

"You go to hell. And besides that, I need to go outside."

"Write the letter first, Mr. Barrett."

"I ain't writing you no damned letter, you son of a bitch. Are you holding me hostage? Is that what this is all about? Are you planning on holding my brothers up for money? Well, I can tell you right now, they won't pay you. They won't pay one red cent, so you're wasting your time. When I get out of here, I'm going to have every one of you bastards killed. That includes you, Tom Hunter, and you, too, Robert Goodman."

Longarm sighed. He said, "All right. Take him back to his room."

Barrett suddenly gripped the sides of the chair he was sitting in and said, "No! No! No! I want something to eat and I want some more water and I want some coffee and I want a drink and I want to go outside."

Longarm looked at him for a long moment. "Well, maybe that last one ain't such a bad idea. Tom, you and Mr. Goodman escort our friend outside. Keep a close eye on him, though I doubt he'll do much running."

Longarm sat there waiting until Archie Barrett reentered through the back door. He had shed his coat and his vest was open and he had taken off his tie and his collar.

Motioning at the writing paraphernalia, Longarm said, "You ready to oblige me now with this letter?"

Barrett looked at him cunningly. He said, "I want something to eat first. I smell bacon. I'd like some bacon and eggs."

"After you write the letter, Mr. Barrett."

The squat man flared up, jerking back his shoulders. He said, "You may think you're tough, but you ain't near as tough as I am. You son of a bitch, I'll finish you before it's all over with."

Longarm nodded at Tom Hunter. "Put him back in his

room and this time, don't be so careful. You don't need to handle him so cautiously, if you take my meaning.''

He sat back down in the chair behind him and listened to the sounds of the commotion coming from the other room. Even as thick as the walls were, Longarm could hear the sounds of blows and of screams. In a moment, Tom Hunter and Goodman were back. Tom Hunter was flexing his right hand. His knuckles looked bruised.

Longarm said, ''Mr. Barrett didn't fall down, did he?''

Tom Hunter smiled faintly. He said, ''Yeah, tripped over the sill of the room right there. Took a bad spill. I hate it when a guest in my house has that kind of misfortune.''

''Has he got water?''

Goodman said, ''That's the bad thing about it. When he fell, he knocked over the table where his pitcher and pan were. Spilled every drop of water on the floor.''

''Somebody ought to take him some more one of these days,'' said Longarm.

Hunter said, ''I'll get to it, right away. First, I need to go outside and see about my cattle.''

Goodman stood up. He said, ''Reckon I do, too.''

''Y'all don't get in a hurry, hear?'' Longarm said. ''By the way, send Rufus in here. I want to ask him about his trip into town.''

Rufus Goodman had just returned from hauling a load of water from a little nearby spring where Tom Hunter got his household water. It wasn't a big enough supply for his cattle. They had to be driven several miles farther on to a little creek that was threatening to go dry. Of course, none of this would have been necessary had Barrett not dammed up Hunter's main stream that ran so close to the house. They brought the water in for the horses. They were all being kept in the barn, out of sight from any curious passersby. That way, it appeared that only Tom Hunter was home alone. Longarm had

122

cautioned that every man should keep himself well concealed.

The young man came in, and Longarm questioned him about what he had heard in town. Young Goodman shrugged his shoulders and said he hadn't heard a word about Archie Barrett. "But then I don't reckon I would, Marshal. They kind of keep their business close up to themselves. It'll be a few days before it gets around town that something's wrong."

Longarm nodded and sent the boy back so he could finish up his chore of watering the horses. After that, he settled back to think. Barrett was going to be a tougher nut to crack than he'd imagined, but crack he would. Longarm had no doubt of it, even if meant that he would personally have to go into the room and talk to Barrett.

That night at supper, Tom Hunter said, "Now, I understand that you want Archie Barrett to write a note to Jake Myers. How are you going to get that note to him?"

Longarm looked up. He said, "Why, the simplest way possible. Deputy Hawkins is going to take it."

Hawkins's mouth fell open. "*Deputy* Hawkins! Let me tell you what, Marshal Long. Deputy Hawkins is fixing to resign and become Mr. Hawkins again, pretty damned quick, and get on about his business of peddling various kinds of leather."

Longarm gave him a mild look. He said, "Now, George, you know there's nobody else that can take that note. None of us can take it. We'd have to rope and drag a Barrett man up here and convince him to take it. It's the most natural thing in the world for Archie Barrett to send that note with you. Can't you all see that?"

Everybody nodded but Hawkins, who said, "Now, damn it, Longarm. I ain't got no desire to go into that armed camp.

I went into one for you and got out alive. I sure as hell don't want to press my luck."

Longarm nodded his head and said, "George, I've got faith in you. I know that you'll do the right thing when the time comes. But let's don't study on it right now. First we've got to get that note out of old Archie. He's being damned stubborn about this matter. I may have to talk to him myself."

Goodman said, "I'd appreciate it if you'd let Rufus here have the next conversation with him. Rufus is real fond of Archie Barrett, aren't you, boy?"

The younger Goodman said, "Yes, sir, Pa. I'm just real fond of him. I'd take great pleasure in speaking to him, especially in a closed room."

Rufus Goodman had been able to find smoked ham in town and they were having that and canned tomatoes and canned peaches. Robert Goodman had turned out to be a first-class biscuit maker and they were also having baking powder biscuits. Tom Hunter claimed it was the first decent meal he'd had since his wife had left.

Longarm said, "Well, it's a good thing. I don't know if I could have kept this crew on the job if we'd had much more of your corn bread and that crispy stuff you call bacon. Have you ever heard of taking it off the fire before it turned into charcoal?"

Tom Hunter laughed good-naturedly. He said, "Well, my wife gave me about two hours of instruction in cooking before she left. I guess she must have left out a few things."

Longarm asked, "Did anybody see any riders today that were more than the common number?"

Robert Goodman and Tom Hunter looked at each other. Both men shook their heads. Hunter said, "I didn't see any extra activity, Marshal, but then, it's still a little early. I don't think they know which way to look. They might have been looking around to the west or in town. No, you said Rufus here didn't hear anything in town. But you can bet they'll be coming and not in the distant future, either. I don't figure we've got forever to get what you want out of Barrett.''

Longarm said, ''Well, I reckon we'd better start standing watches tonight. It shouldn't be any hardship. We'll cut it up into about eight hours and each man can watch about two hours. I'm deliberately letting Mr. Hawkins out of that duty because I'm going to have to call on him for that extra-special job of work of carrying the note to Myers, if we ever get it. So, it'll just be the four of us doing two hours each, and I'll take the first one, beginning at eleven o'clock. That ought to see us through dawn. One thing that y'all have to be certain of and that is not to give anybody that's spying up here any reason to think that there's anything unusual going on. There's more here than normally would be here, so let's not bunch up. I know you've got to see to your cattle and I know you've got to herd them, but young Rufus ought to be able to handle that. I think the rest of us should try to stay out of sight as much as possible. I know I am.''

Hunter said, ''What about Barrett? When are we going to give another little glimmer?''

Longarm said, ''I reckon first thing in the morning. I don't reckon he's going to spend a very comfortable night, seeing as how he's out of water. He ought to be getting pretty hungry by now, and he ain't yelling anywhere near as loud as he was yesterday. He seems to be running out of wind.''

Tom Hunter said, ''Reckon we ought to have knocked a little more out of him?''

Longarm shook his head. He said, ''Tom you can carry that stuff too far. It'll even get a coward's back up, if you bruise him up too much and he figures he ain't got anything to lose. No, we're going to work on Mr. Barrett's mind. See, he don't know that we've got plans for him. He don't know anything. All he knows is that he's hungry, he's thirsty, and he's uncomfortable. He don't know what the hell has happened and that unknown thing is what's bothering him most of all. If you beat on a man, you can stiffen his backbone more than you think. I figure he'll be most vulnerable at first light, so when we're all up, we'll have another go at it and see what happens.''

Longarm spent his watch sitting out in front of the cabin gazing across the moonlit range. It was a pretty sight. He could make out a few lights still on in town, and he wondered how Mrs. Thompson was getting along. She was going to be a very instrumental part of this plan, and for her sake, he desperately hoped it would work. In the short time he had known her, he'd grown fond of her and he'd come to admire her. If for no other reason than her welfare, he intended to bring peace to the area and to pull the teeth of the big bully families that had been causing so much trouble. She was a fine woman and did not deserve the sadness that had been brought into her life. He hoped, for her sake and for his, that the business could be wound up very quickly. There were some parts of his plan he didn't understand because he didn't know the ins and outs of certain parts of it, but he figured that either she did or Hawkins did or somebody did and he'd just follow their advice. What he needed now were the two ringleaders in his custody and at his mercy. After that, he thought things might well go along the right path.

Everyone was up a little before seven. Tom Hunter put a big pot of coffee on to brew and started some bacon frying mainly for Archie Barrett's benefit. Then Longarm set the paper and the ink bottle and the pen out on the table again and sent the older Goodman and his son to fetch Archie Barrett.

Barrett looked worse than he had the day before, which was what Longarm had expected. His clothes were in disarray and a grubby black growth of whiskers was sprouting. He came into the room working his mouth and saying, "Water! Water! I've got to have some water. I'm dying of thirst."

Longarm nodded at the paper and the pen. He said, "All you've got to do, Mr. Barrett, to get some water and a meal, is to pick up that pen and write what I tell you. Set him in that chair, Mr. Goodman."

They guided Barrett into the chair and Robert Goodman held the pen out to him. He looked at it for a moment and then tentatively reached for it. He looked up at Longarm. Longarm could tell from his eyes there was still plenty of fight left in him.

"What the hell do you think I'm supposed to write?" Barrett said.

"Dip the pen in the ink and start off by saying, 'Jake Myers.' Just write that down, not 'Dear Jake' or 'To Jake Myers.' Just write down 'Jake Myers' and I'll tell you the rest."

Barrett stared at the paper and then stared at Longarm. He said, "I don't know what the hell you're trying to pull, but I ain't going to have no part of it." With a sudden move, he swept his hand across the table, striking the bottle of ink. It slid to the edge and would have tipped over except for the quick hands of Rufus Goodman. He caught it just off the stone floor. It would have broken for certain and that would have meant another trip to town for more ink.

Longarm shook his head. "Barrett, you ain't making yourself very popular around here." He glanced over at Rufus. "Son, did any of that ink spill?" he said.

"Yes, sir. There's a pretty good splotch on the floor. I tried to catch it in time, but it was canted sideways and about half of it spilled out."

Longarm sighed. He said, "Barrett, I'm sorry as hell that you did that. Now, take your shirt off and mop up Mr. Hunter's floor. He don't want folks staining it with ink. Understand me?''

Barrett glared at him. He said, "Go to hell."

Longarm nodded at Hunter. He said, "Mr. Hunter, would you and Mr. Goodman assist Mr. Barrett in taking off his shirt and help him mop that ink up? Get him down on his hands and knees. Might be his face would be the best thing to wipe that spot instead of his shirt."

With rough hands, they stripped the vest and then the white shirt off Archie Barrett. Then, holding him by both arms, they hustled him out of the chair and then bent him over until his face was touching the floor. Longarm's view was blocked by the table, but he could see them making swabbing motions with Archie Barrett's upper body. Finally, he said, "All right. That's enough."

They brought Archie Barrett back up and plumped him into the chair. Longarm noticed that he was hairy all over his body. He said, "Mister Barrett, now I know why you act like a gorilla. My God, I've never seen a man with so much hair in all my life. You need to shave your back."

Barrett's face was a mess. Hunter and Goodman had not been as careful as they could have been about putting Barrett's shirt between his face and the ink. A good deal of the ink had been smeared down one side of his cheek and his forehead and into his hair. The shirt was a mess.

Barrett said sullenly, "You son of a bitch, you'll pay for this one of these days."

Longarm said, "No, Mr. Barrett, you're going to pay. You are going to pay and pay and pay and then pay back what you've stolen from these people. Understand that?" He leaned across the table so that Barrett could get the full implication of his words. "I'm glad you brought up the word *pay,* because you ain't got no idea how much you and Jake Myers owe these folks, and I'm going to see that you pay back every damned cent. Take him back to his room, boys, and this time, don't be quite so gentle."

As they pulled Barrett up, he said, "Wait a minute, damn it. Wait a minute."

Longarm said, "What?"

Barrett stared at the blank sheet of paper and the pen. Then he looked up at Longarm. "What do you want me to write to Jake Myers?"

"I want you to invite him to a rendezvous with you. I want you to tell him that you want to have a meeting with him."

"Why would I want to have a meeting with Jake Myers?"

"You want to have a meeting about me. About a deputy U.S. marshal who is stirring up trouble. You want to talk about doing something about me."

"Why would he come?"

Longarm said, "Because he's already worried about me, that's why. I've already killed two of his men, maybe more; I don't know. I've lost track."

Barrett stared at him. His little pig eyes bored straight ahead into Longarm's face. He said, "You think you're pretty tough, don't you mister?"

Longarm shook his head. He said, "No, I don't think I'm tough. I think I'm doing my job. Now, do you want to write that letter and then get some water and some of that bacon that's frying over there?"

The room began to fill with the mouth-watering smell of the bacon. In a little while, Longarm knew, it would smell like burned bacon if Tom Hunter was kept on as cook, but for the time being it smelled good. Longarm said, "What's it going to be? Speak now. I ain't got time to fool with you."

Barrett shook loose from Goodman and Hunter. He said, "Give me the damned pen and ink." Rufus Goodman was holding the bottle of ink and the pen. He set them in front of Archie Barrett.

Barrett picked up the pen and then dipped it into the ink. He looked up at Longarm and said, "You swear you'll give me water and something to eat if I write this, and then you'll turn me loose?"

Longarm said, "I'm not going to swear anything to you, Mr. Barrett. I promise you this and I'll swear this to you, you're going back into that room until you rot if you don't write. That's what I will swear to you. So, you make up your mind about it."

Barrett's voice took on a whine. He said, "I don't see what you need with me after I write this letter. You ought to be willing to turn me loose. If I write it, you ought to be through with me."

"What are you doing, Mr. Barrett? Reading my mind? You don't know what's in my mind. Now, you write what I tell you, and I'll give you some water and some breakfast. That's all I'll promise you. It's your choice: either write or go back in that room."

Barrett's face grew sullen. He glanced around at the hard-looking men standing around him. Finally, he dipped his pen again in the ink and then wrote the name *Jake Myers* at the top. After that, he looked up at Longarm, the pen poised in his hand. He said, "Now what?"

Longarm said, "Write what I tell you."

Myers, I think to have a meeting about this here United States marshal that has come to town and is causing quite a bit of trouble. I hear he has been interfering in your business and I damned sure know he's been interfering in mine. I'm sending this note by that leather peddler Hawkins who has been over here trying to sell me a saddle. He says he is on his way to your place. I figure we should meet this afternoon about three o'clock at the rocky hill just east of town. I figure that's about halfway between us. I won't be bringing any men with me.

We've had our differences in the past, but I figure we need to handle this one with a common interest. Once he's dealt with, we can take up where we left off, but until that time, I'm willing to call a truce between us. If you can't come at three o'clock, send me a note back by that saddle salesman.

Longarm waited until Barrett had finished writing. He had to admit that the man wrote a damned good hand.

When Barrett had finished the last sentence, he looked up. Longarm said, "Just sign your name. Archie Barrett."

When the document was complete, Longarm took it up and read it carefully, looking for any tricks or hidden meanings. There were none. Barrett had taken it down exactly as he had spoken it.

Barrett said, a little croak in his voice, "Now, what about some water and some whiskey and something to eat?"

Longarm grinned at him. He said, "You know, Mr. Barrett, you expect us now to treat you fair and decent, like we're going to keep our part of the bargain because you've kept yours. Well, I don't think we're going to do that, Barrett. We're going to treat you the way you've been treating these folks around here for years. You can have some breakfast and you can have some water and you can have some coffee—you can't have no whiskey—but you can only have it after we've had our breakfast. Mr. Hunter and Mr. Goodman, would y'all escort Mr. Archie Barrett back to his room?"

It gave Longarm a deep inside chuckle to hear Barrett scream and curse as he was thrown once again into the room and have the heavy door shut on him. When Hunter and Goodman came back, Longarm rubbed his hands together. He said, "Well, gentlemen, let's get this thing started. Let's have some breakfast. I believe we can even have some eggs, courtesy of young Mr. Goodman here and his endeavors. Mr.

Goodman, if you'll fry up a good batch of eggs and keep Tom out of the kitchen and make up some more of those baking powder biscuits, we'll have a good feed.''

He glanced over at Hawkins. ''Then Deputy George Hawkins will be off on his mission to carry this little missive to our good friend, Jake Myers.''

Hawkins just gave Longarm a sour look and got up to pour himself a cup of coffee. He said as he passed, ''You know I wouldn't do this, Marshal, if the pay wasn't right. I'd do nearly anything for two dollars a day.''

Longarm smiled. He said, ''That's the spirit, Mr. Hawkins. By the way, do you know where this rocky hill is?''

Hawkins said, ''Of course. If you recall, I was the one who suggested it. I probably know this country better than any one person around here. Lord knows I've been all over it.''

While they had waited for Barrett to agree to write the note, Longarm had questioned the others about a possible rendezvous point that would also give him a place of ambush. A small hill with rocky outcroppings had been chosen, mainly because about a mile farther north there was a small butte with some little caves that led into it. It would make an ideal place for Longarm to await the coming of Jake Myers and Hawkins.

From the kitchen, Hawkins said, ''In that letter you got Barrett telling Myers to come alone. I can guarantee you, Marshal Long, that Jake Myers ain't going to stir his fat old ass out into the open without a couple, three gunhands with him. That's for sure.''

Longarm said, ''Well, if that's the way it has to be, that's the way it's got to be. You just make sure you ain't amongst them, that you have business back in town.''

They ate their breakfast and then Tom Hunter and the elder Mr. Goodman went to get Archie Barrett out and feed and water him. While they were at the task, Longarm beckoned Hawkins out the front door. They walked a little way from the cabin, surveying the range that led back down toward the town. Longarm said, "Look here, George, if you're really not of mind to deliver that note to Mr. Myers, I can understand it. I don't want to ask you to do something you don't really want to do, because I figure you've already done more than I could ask of any citizen, luring Mr. Barrett out from behind his fort where I could get my hands on him."

George Hawkins smiled slightly. He said, "Well, that's mighty kind of you, Marshal, though I think you're just trying to salve your own conscience. If I don't take that note, who do you reckon is going to take it? Tom Hunter? Rufus Goodman? Robert Goodman? I don't think so. Why don't you just take it yourself? It would be just about the same as if you sent one of them."

"You could go into town and find some young boy and pay him a couple dollars to take it out there."

Hawkins laughed. He said, "Yeah, and the first thing Jake Myers is going to ask that boy is, 'Who gave you that note, son? I'm going to twist your arm off and shove it up your ass.' And that kid would describe me and then Mr. Myers would know." He shook his head. "No, there ain't but one way, and that's for me to stick my head in the lion's den again, like it or not. Why all this, Marshal? Are you getting worried about me?"

"No, I can't say that I'm getting worried about you, George. It's just that you bitch such an uncommon much when you're asked to do the least little old thing, like just make a short five-mile ride and drop off a note and come back."

Hawkins looked Longarm steadily in the eye. He said, "You want this note put in Myers's hands, don't you?"

"Yep."

133

"You don't want it handed off to some hired hand and then I turn tail and run, do you?"

"Nope."

"So, then I'll be standing there while Jake Myers reads it. Right?" Hawkins said.

"Right."

"And you reckon he's going to let me take off?"

Longarm took a second to answer. Finally, he said, "I don't see why not."

Hawkins laughed. "Then you're a bigger damfool than I thought. Listen, this time, don't shoot so damned close to me. That's all I ask."

"You ain't got no idea what I'm going to do," Longarm said.

Hawkins spit on the ground and scuffed at it with the toe of his boot. He said, "Marshal, I've done seen you in action. I know how you do your talking. Now, let's go back in. I could do with another cup of coffee."

Longarm turned around and glanced inside the cabin. He could see that Barrett was still at the table. He said, "Let's wait a minute until that pig gets out of there. I can't stand the sight of him."

Hawkins cackled. He said, "He is a sight, isn't he. That's the hairiest son of a bitch I believe I've ever seen. What we ought to have done, or maybe still could do, is hold him over a low fire and turn him and singe all that hair off of him. Wouldn't do no good shaving it, it'd just grow back."

Longarm said, "Mr. Hawkins, you do have the best ideas. Are you sure you want to do this?"

Hawkins looked at him with amazement in his face. "Want to do it? Hell, no, I don't want to do it. But will I do it? Hell, yes, I'll do it. You just be damned sure you do your part."

Longarm said with a straight face, "I'll go inside and get

about a half of a bottle of whiskey in me so as to steady my hand. How's that? That make you feel better?''

Hawkins stared at him with round eyes. He said, ''Don't be saying that to an old reformed drunk. My God, man. You scare me to death talking like that. I better not even see you near a bottle of whiskey.''

''Oh, I won't be near a bottle. I'll put it in a glass if that makes you feel any better.''

Hawkins said, ''You are a rare son of a bitch, Marshal.''

Longarm answered, ''No, I call myself more well done than rare.''

Chapter 9

They had all calculated that it was about a two-hour ride for Hawkins to Jake Myers's ranch and a little over an hour's ride for Longarm to the butte where he could take up his ambush position on the northern side of the knoll they called Rocky Hill, the place the note suggested that Barrett and Jake Myers meet. Hawkins was fidgety and anxious to get it over with, so they sent him off at about eleven o'clock, allowing him to take it slow and easy so as to arrive around one o'clock and hope that he could get Myers started no later than two. Longarm planned to give himself plenty of time. He was going to start for his position no later than noon.

Rufus Goodman had Longarm's horse saddled and bridled and had made sure that the saddle blanket was smooth and that the roan's hooves were clean with no stones or any other objects that could make the gelding go lame. Longarm's preparations were to put a dozen rifle cartridges into his shirt pocket and to stick his extra .44-caliber revolver in his belt. It might be uncomfortable, but then he couldn't be sure when he was going to need it. Hunter urged him to take along a 12-gauge, double-barreled shotgun that Hunter owned, but Longarm said, "If I let anybody get that close, I'll go to fighting him with the butt end of my pistol."

The others had watched Hawkins ride away. Longarm came back inside and sat down at the table. There wasn't a whole hell of a lot to say. Either Myers came and they could go ahead with their plan, or he wouldn't. There was nothing they could do about it.

Longarm said, "Did our star boarder make a good breakfast?"

Robert Goodman shook his head. He said, "I damned near couldn't cook fast enough, the way that son of a bitch was poking it down, and he must have drank about a half of gallon of water and about the same amount of coffee. Then he had the nerve to want whiskey."

Longarm shook his head. "I'm glad I wasn't here to see it."

Tom Hunter said, "He ain't a very pretty sight, I've got to admit that. I don't know how long it's going to take me to get that room clean and smelling like anything."

Longarm stood up, yawned, and walked to the door. The figure of Hawkins was a mere dot in the distance as he traveled toward the northwest. He turned back into the room. He said, "I guess I'd better think about getting ready to go." He found the bottle of whiskey where he had left it in the kitchen and poured himself a half a glass. He put some water in it to make it last longer and then began sipping.

Mr. Goodman looked at him curiously. He said, "You pretty fond of that stuff, Marshal."

Longarm shook his head. He said, "No, I drink it under doctor's orders."

"Doctor's orders? What doctor ordered you to drink whiskey?"

Longarm said, "I never got his name. He was shaking so bad, with me pointing a gun at him, that he could barely write out the instructions of how much whiskey I was supposed to drink every day."

They all laughed, though not very loud. They were all nervous and worried.

Tom Hunter stood up from the table. He had strapped on a gun belt with a revolver in a deep holster. He was obviously no gunman. He said, "Marshal, don't you reckon it might be a good idea if I went with you to try and stop Myers? I can guarantee you he ain't coming by himself. You'll have two, three, maybe more to deal with. You might could use some help."

Longarm shook his head. "I'm sure you're a good and capable man, Tom. I'm sure you're a very capable man at a lot of things, but this is the kind of business I've had a lot of experience in. Hawkins, bless his soul, might be in the middle of that bunch, and I'd rather it just be me doing the shooting. Nothing said against you, understand?"

"I catch your drift, and you're probably right."

"Beside that," Longarm said. "If they get through me, there's an excellent chance they might make straight for here. If that's the case, you're going to need all the guns you can muster. So I think it's better if you stay here, Tom, as well as young Rufus and Mr. Goodman."

He looked over at the young man. He said, "My horse ready, Rufus?"

"Yes, sir. He's as ready as he's going to get."

Longarm got out his watch and looked at it. He said, "Then I reckon it's time for me to be starting. Do we have a canteen handy? It might get a little warm out there, waiting."

Rufus said, "I've already hung one on your saddle horn, Marshal. It ain't but a gallon canteen, but it ought to do ya. Do you want to take along any grub?"

Longarm said, "I don't reckon this is the kind of job that a man needs to take along his lunch. This ought to be over pretty quick. Well, I'll be going now." He gave them a nod and walked out the front door. He could feel the others coming out behind him. Without looking back, he mounted his roan gelding and reined him around toward the northwest.

Behind him, Tom Hunter said, "You'll see Rocky Hill pretty quick after you go over a rise and down a valley and then up another rise. You can't miss it. Then it's about a mile on past that to that butte where you'll be taking up your position."

Longarm looked around at them. He said, "Keep our guest happy, and I'll see if I can't bring us in another boarder." They mumbled and nodded and shuffled their feet and gave him a wave as he put the spurs to the roan and left at a high lope.

The butte was almost ideal for Longarm's purposes. He was able to hide his horse behind a little rocky outcropping that was almost like a cave. He could peer around a ledge and have a clear view to the northwest toward the Myerses' ranch where he hoped Jake Myers and George Hawkins would be coming from and coming soon. His watch said one o'clock and he was starting to worry. They should have been in sight.

He sat in the shade at the feet of his horse and took a little nip of whiskey and smoked a cigarillo. There was no one in sight to spot the slight trail of smoke that was drifting upward. He could only hope that Hawkins and the note were bait enough to fetch the big fish out of his little pond. Every ten minutes or so, he glanced around the ledge, hoping to see something. There was nothing the first several times he looked.

Finally, at one thirty, he was able to distinguish a group of black dots coming from the proper direction and heading his way. He took one more swallow of whiskey and put it back in his saddlebag, buckled it shut, and then took a drink of water out of the canteen. It had become lukewarm in the afternoon sunshine, but it was wet. He looked again. The dots were much closer, and there were more of them than he had hoped there would be. They had not come close enough yet for him to take a count, but he knew with a sinking heart that there were more than two or three. This, he thought, was going to be tougher than he expected.

He put a boot in his stirrup and mounted his horse, pulling him back farther behind the ledge. He took off his hat and peered around the edge of the rock. Now the riders were only a half mile to a mile off. As best he could, he could count six and there might have even been a seventh. He couldn't tell who they were. Longarm wouldn't have known Jake Myers if they had been in a poker game together, but he felt certain he would recognize the easy riding style of Hawkins.

Longarm got ready by tying a knot in his reins and dropping them behind the saddle horn. It appeared it would be a two-hand job, and he'd have to guide his pony with his knees. The horse had been well trained and he had no doubt that it would work out like that.

He took one last look and saw that the riders were only three or four hundred yards off. Now, he could see them clearly. Up front and in the middle was a big, heavyset man wearing a white Stetson hat and a gray beard. He was plump and heavy and looked to be at least sixty years old. Longarm had little doubt that the man was Jake Myers. Then he saw George Hawkins, riding a little behind and to the right of

Myers. His heart sank as he counted the outriders. There were five of them, five gunmen. He was certain of that. Well, this was going to take some doing, he thought. He guessed that it might scare Hawkins a little more than Hawkins cared to be scared, but he didn't know how else to go about it. He got his Winchester up out of the boot and got set, pulling back slightly on the reins to let the horse know that they were fixing to do something. He listened rather than looked. He could hear the hoofbeats of the horses going at a fast trot as they neared and then as they passed.

As they passed, he swung his horse out and put the spurs to him and circled the rock to his left, keeping on around the butte until he was in behind the party. He was some hundred or hundred and fifty yards behind them, but he didn't care. It was going to be difficult shooting, but he thought he could manage it. He lifted his horse up into a slow gallop and raised up in his stirrups and threw the Winchester to his shoulder. He hated to shoot horses, but he didn't know any other way outside of shooting the men in the back, and he wasn't going to do that. What he hoped to do was burn the horses with a shot across the rump, enough to either cripple them temporarily or cause them to buck and change direction, perhaps throwing their riders.

Longarm got off the first shot on the man trailing and he saw immediately that the tactic might work. The horse suddenly veered to his right and began pitching. It caught the rider so off guard that he went tumbling off, going head over feet, sprawling on the rocky ground.

They didn't seem to have heard the shot, and Longarm levered in another cartridge and aimed at the horse next in line. He fired again and this time the horse stumbled, his hindquarters sagging. Longarm feared he had wounded the horse too deeply, but by then, he had no time to look. Already, he had thrown a fresh shell into the chamber and had fired at the third horse. It instantly went down in a heap, rolling over the rider and pinning him. By now, the other four riders were aware that they were under fire. Myers was to the far left. Beside him, and trying to drop back, rode Hawkins. There were two gunmen to the right of the leather salesman, all looking backward.

Longarm didn't like them so close to Hawkins. It was going to be a hard shot from about seventy yards off a running horse, but he stood up in his stirrups and aimed carefully at the gunman nearest George Hawkins. He squeezed off a shot and saw the man suddenly pitch forward and then slowly slide down the side of his galloping horse. The other man fired off a revolver shot that went over Longarm's head. Longarm was coming up on the first of the men whose horses he had disabled. The man was still down, but he was scrambling to pick up a revolver. Longarm couldn't afford to waste another rifle cartridge as he only had one left and he didn't have time to reload. He quickly flipped the Winchester from his right hand to his left and drew his revolver and fired at the man from about five yards away as he closed on him rapidly. The bullet caught the man somewhere near the middle of his chest, and he whirled around and fell forward.

The next man was still under his horse, but at that instant, Longarm saw real danger. The third man he'd dropped was clear of his horse and had somehow managed to get his rifle in his hands. He was squatting there on one knee, leveling down, trying to bring his sights to bear on Longarm. There was no time to shoot carefully. The man was thirty or forty yards away, which was a very long shot for a pistol. All Longarm could do was thumb the big .44 revolver and fire as fast as he could. The man got off one rifle shot and it sang right by Longarm's ear. The third shot Longarm fired took the man in the belly. He doubled over, dropping his rifle, and fell on his side.

Now there was no more time to be concerned about those that were left. It was time to get the last of the gunmen, get Hawkins loose, and take Jake Myers into custody. He had the one cartridge left in his Winchester, and putting the spurs to his horse, he closed the distance to thirty yards before he raised up to fire at the last man. The man was turned in his saddle, firing rapidly with a revolver. Longarm shot him just under the shoulder. The bullet knocked him across the side of the saddle. For a second, he hung down among the thrashing hooves of his horse. Then he slipped away, falling to the ground and went tumbling end over end over end.

In that instant, Hawkins suddenly split away to the right, leaving only Jake Myers riding alone. As Longarm gained on him, he could see the old fat man giving frightened looks over his shoulder. Their horses were both in a dead run, but Longarm's had much the easier load, and within ten jumps, Longarm was almost up to the tail of Myers's horse. He could see Myers fumbling inside his pocket for some kind of weapon. He didn't want to shoot the man—it would defeat his purpose—so he swerved his horse over until he was right behind the old man and his mount. The man was too stout to turn far enough around in his saddle to fire, and Longarm knew that his horse wasn't going to be able to run much farther, carrying such a load. To get Myers's attention, Longarm pulled the extra revolver out of his waistband and, aiming carefully, shot the white Stetson off the old man's head. It took all the starch out of Myers. His horse was already beginning to slow. Longarm fired another warning shot and then Myers pulled his horse down to a gallop and then a lope and then finally down to a trot. Longarm frantically waved for Hawkins to ride away before he came up alongside Jake Myers.

The old man turned his fat, florid face on Longarm and gave him such a look of fury that Longarm was glad he wasn't carrying a cannon. If he had been, Longarm thought he might have taken great delight in putting a hole through the man. As he came abreast of Myers, he said, making his point with the revolver he was still carrying in his hand, "If you've got any hardware on you, Mr. Myers, or anything that's likely to shoot, you'd better get rid of it right now, or else this thing in my hand is likely to go off."

The old man gave him a disgusted look and then reached into the pocket of his suit coat and came out with a small-caliber revolver and cast it aside.

They slowed to a walk.

Longarm said, "Jake Myers, my name is U.S. Deputy Marshal Custis Long. You are under arrest for various offenses, both federal and state."

Myers's face was furious. He said, "You go to hell."

Longarm said, "Maybe, but first we're going to go up to Tom Hunter's cabin so you can meet and talk to Archie Barrett and he can tell you how comfortable it is living up there."

Jake Myers's voice was unnaturally high for a man of his girth and size. He said, "Let me tell you something, you simpleton son of a bitch, you ain't got any right to arrest me, and before this is all over, you're going to sure as hell wish you hadn't. I've got friends, plenty of friends. They'll probably not only have your job, they'll probably have your ass."

Longarm reached out and grabbed the bridle of Jake Myers's horse and brought them both to a stop. He said, "Let's me and you get something straight right quick, Myers. Nothing about you scares me. In fact, there's nothing about you that makes me feel anything at all except disgust. You've had it all your way around here for far too long, and you've made a lot of folks miserable as hell. But all that's over with now. There's nothing you could do to me, but I'm going to

144

do plenty to you. Let's get that straight. I'm a United States deputy marshal and you can't touch me.''

Myers glared at him for a moment and then waved a hand at the departing figure of George Hawkins. He said, "There goes a Judas goat. I'll hang that son of a bitch, that's for sure. He's the one who lured me into your trap.''

Longarm said, "That man has been sworn in as a deputy United States marshal, same as me. You touch one hair on his head, and you'll never see so much trouble in all your life. There'll be five hundred deputy marshals come boiling down around this place, and there won't be a thing left of this countryside once they get through. Matter of fact, nothing will grow here for ten years once they get through, and that includes you. Now, you might as well make your mind up to the fact that things have changed and there's not a damned thing you can do about it. Let's get to making some tracks for Tom Hunter's cabin. We've got some business to do today. I'm as sick of this whole affair as I've ever been of any job I've ever had since I became a marshal. I'd like to get it over with and get out of here and away from the likes of you and Archie Barrett. Get that damned horse moving, that is if he can carry your fat gut the mile or two more we've got to go.''

As they rode, Myers said only one thing and that was to ask Longarm if he had intentionally set up an ambush for him.

Longarm said, "Hell, no, Myers. I've been watching for you to come out of your lair for some time. It was just an accident that you came along at just the time I was hiding behind that butte. Just one of those lucky coincidences. I'm sorry about your men. Seems like several of them had horses step into gopher holes and fall over.''

The fat man turned in his saddle and glared again at Longarm. He said, "I don't know how I'm going to do it, but I'm going to fix your wagon."

Longarm smiled. "My wagon ain't broke, Myers. Now, get moving."

Just before they got to Tom Hunter's cabin, Myers said, "I don't know what you got in mind, marshal, but I do know you can't stay here forever, and when you leave, things'll get straightened back out again."

"Mr. Myers, you know that very thought occurred to me. An idea came to me in the middle of the night and I went to thinking about it and I've kind of got it figured out how things aren't going to go back to where they were after I leave. I think I've got a way where we can get you and Mr. Barrett to be good to your neighbors. You reckon?"

Myers's only reaction was to give Longarm another one of his glares. Longarm calculated that the man could make as ugly a face as anyone he had ever seen.

As they came riding up to the door of the cabin, Tom Hunter and the Goodmans came crowding out, their faces alight with smiles. The Goodmans practically dragged Jake Myers out of his saddle. He was their principal meat, since they were convinced that it was his men who had burned them out and stolen their cattle. Longarm dismounted, loosened the cinch on his horse's saddle, untied the knot in the reins, and let them fall to the ground. He figured young Rufus would tend to the horses in due time after he got through helping Myers into the cabin. Tom Hunter stood silently by the door, looking pleased. As Longarm came up, he stuck out his hand and they shook.

Tom Hunter said, "Congratulations, Marshal. Was it easy?"

"About like falling off a log. That is, a log straight up and you don't want to fall off a log straight up."

"He have any men with him?"

146

"Five."

Hunter whistled softly. He said, "And what did they have to say about the matter?"

Longarm shook his head. "I don't know," he said. "They kept falling off their horses. I don't know what was the matter with them. I'd be damned if I'd hire men like that. Couldn't ride for sour grapes. I think some of them hurt themselves when they fell, too."

Tom Hunter smiled faintly. "That's a shame."

Longarm could see that Tom Hunter was not a cruel man, but he couldn't blame the rancher for taking some small satisfaction in seeing a little of it coming back his way.

When Longarm got into the main room of the cabin, they had Myers sitting down at the table with his coat off and his shirt undone.

Longarm stopped and looked puzzled. "Y'all fixing to bathe him? I agree he smells a little bit, but this is going a little too far."

Robert Goodman said grimly, "This is a tricky son of a bitch." He held out his hand and showed Longarm a derringer. "And I wouldn't be surprised if he doesn't have another one somewhere around on his person."

Longarm looked at Myers. He said, "Damn it, Jake. I'm surprised at you. Didn't I tell you to get rid of any hardware or anything that might make an explosion or that might shoot somebody? Well, I'm amazed that you didn't listen to me. I've got a good mind to never let you have a gun ever again. Yeah, I reckon y'all had better search him all the way. But for God's sake, don't take all his clothes off. I don't think any of us could stand the sight. I wish I had cattle as fat as he is."

Tom Hunter said, "Ain't that the truth. Lord, a man could retire if he had a hundred head carrying that much weight."

Longarm went into the kitchen and poured himself a glass

of whiskey and stood leaning against the counter, sipping it, while he lit a cigarillo. When he had that going good, he turned and asked the group if they were satisfied that Myers had no further weapons.

Goodman nodded. He gestured toward a small pile on the table. He said, "That's all he's got. Some coins, his wallet, a penknife, and his watch."

Longarm said, "Well, chuck him back in that room with his old buddy. He and old Archie ought to have quite a bit to talk about."

Tom Hunter and Ralph Goodman took Jake Myers by the arms and lifted him out of the chair. He began to protest immediately, but he might as well have been talking to rocks for all the attention they paid him. They manhandled him across the space of the big middle room and then unlocked the door and shoved him through. Longarm could hear Myers yelling and shouting and then suddenly shut up. Longarm thought he'd probably seen Archie Barrett and the surprise had taken the words out of his mouth.

Hunter and Goodman came back from their chore. Hunter said, "Now what, Marshal?"

Longarm walked over to the table and sat down. He said, "Now, I've got to do some writing. I ain't real good at this word stuff, though I ought to be, as many reports as I've had to turn into my boss, who, by the way, is about twice as mean as both of them sons of bitches put together."

Robert Goodman said, "What are you going to write, Marshal? You haven't really filled us in on all the details."

Longarm yawned. He said, "I think you'll understand it better after I get it finished."

Tom Hunter said, "Marshal, we're all proud of you, dragging them two big shots in here, but I still ain't quite certain how we're going to use it to our advantage."

148

"Never you mind, Tom. I think we can use it to our advantage. It's the only hope I can think of."

Rufus came in from putting the horses up. He was all excited and eager. He said, "Marshal, did you know there's some blood on the front of your horse and it ain't from your horse? Must have shot somebody up so close, it splattered on it."

Longarm smiled slightly. "Did you wash it off?"

"Yes, sir, I did, but I was just wondering how it come to be there."

The young man's father looked at him. He said, "Rufus, sometimes you talk too much. Sometimes you ask too many questions."

Longarm said, "No, that's all right. That's the only way the boy's going to learn." He turned to Rufus, "Yeah, I had to shoot a guy at about five yards as I was closing on him at a gallop. I was firing my handgun. He was about halfway raised up. I would guess the bullet I pumped into his lungs spurted some blood out. I wish the son of a bitch hadn't gotten his blood on my horse."

Rufus said almost breathlessly, "How many you kill, Marshal?"

His daddy said sharply, "Rufus, I'll have no more of that. You're starting to sound as bloodthirsty as the men who work for those two in the back room."

"Your daddy's right, Rufus. This ain't anything to be keeping count of, and I don't take no pleasure in that part of my job. I'm a peace officer. I'm not a trouble officer. Unfortunately, sometimes keeping the peace involves having trouble."

Tom Hunter brought Longarm several sheets of clean paper and the pen and ink. Longarm got settled down with his drink and his cigarillo and started in to write. He got so far as "We the Undersigned" and then Hawkins came blowing in through the door.

He was looking exuberant and triumphant and excited. He said, "Boys, I never knowed I had it in me! I really never knew I had it in me!" He looked at Longarm. "That's what I call a good early afternoon piece of work."

"You want me to congratulate you for going into Jake Myers's camp, don't you?"

Hawkins's Adam's apple bobbed up and down. "Hell, yes. I not only went in and got Barrett, but I went in and got Myers, too. Say, do you know how close some of them bullets you were firing came to me?"

Longarm said, "They never came within ten yards of you. Are you going to start that again?"

Hawkins was almost chortling. He said, "That was something. You know, the way you were burning them horses so they'd go to jumping and pitching and then popping them old boys when they were scrambling around on the ground and then the clean way you knocked them other two off."

Longarm looked pained, especially from the expression on Rufus Goodman's face. He said, "By the way, George, you were carrying that .38 caliber pistol of yours. Why the hell didn't you shoot those guys on either side of you? It would have saved me a lot of trouble."

Hawkins looked shocked. He said, "Me? Shoot somebody? I ain't supposed to be shooting anyone. Hell, I'm a leather salesman."

Longarm said, "You're a United States deputy marshal, which gives you the right to shoot anybody I'm shooting at."

Hawkins took off his hat and scratched his head. "You know, I never thought about it that way. I reckon I could have, couldn't I?"

Longarm gave him a flicker of a smile. He said, "You ever shot anybody, George?"

Hawkins thought a moment, then said, "No, I don't reckon I have."

"Then I don't recommend you go to trying it in the future."

Hawkins said, "You know it ain't going to be safe around here for me unless you get Barrett and Myers put plumb away. Of course, they're still going to have kin around here. I guess you know you've ruined this area for me."

Longarm shook his head. "Nope. I've told Jake Myers that you were a United States deputy marshal and you had full right to be doing what you were doing and when I get through with this plan of mine, I don't think Mr. Barrett or Mr. Myers are going to be bothering anybody. Now, why don't you go and get yourself a drink of buttermilk or whiskey and quit bothering me? I've got this here letter to write."

"A letter?"

"Well, it ain't exactly a letter. Let me get on it."

For the next thirty minutes, Longarm laboriously wrote out two documents. It took him so long because he wasn't sure of some of the spelling and he never did write a neat hand, and also, he wanted to get the wording just exactly right. The others stood around watching him somberly, curious but not wanting to break into his mood. The only noise was the yelling and screaming from the back room where Jake Myers and Archie Barrett were confined.

When he was finishing the second document, he said, "Does anybody know what Mrs. Thompson's first name is?"

They looked one to the other. Finally, Hawkins said, "I believe it's Judith. As a matter of fact, I'm certain it's Judith. Why don't you just make it Mrs. Milton Thompson?"

Longarm said, "Yeah, that's probably the best idea."

Longarm sat back, finally satisfied. He looked the two documents over and then he glanced at the four eager faces staring at him. He said, "Do y'all want to hear what these say?"

Tom Hunter said, "Well, I reckon."

Hawkins said, "You're worse than a cat with a mouse. You know we want to know what they say. Lives are at stake here, maybe even my own."

Longarm said, "All right, I'll read the first one. It's a confession. Here's what it says:

"We, the undersigned, Archie Barrett and Jake Myers, freely and willingly confess to causing the murder of Milton Thompson of Grit, Texas. We also confess to the murder and manslaughter of several homesteaders in the Grit area. We further confess and admit to cattle theft, horse theft, and the burning of homes and barns of homesteaders in the same area. We make this confession of our own free will and we give it in the hope that it will cause peace to come to this area. We understand that this confession, given to United States Deputy Marshal Custis Long, stands as a parole for our insuring that no such further incidents will happen in the Grit area. We further pledge ourselves to the fair and open use of water and grazing rights by all parties concerned in this area. No longer will we dam up streams or run cattle off of government free ranges. This parole, we understand, will become a full-fledged confession of our misdeeds should any of the homesteaders in this area suffer any further damages or mischief, either at our hands or the hands of the men who work for us.

Agreed to and signed by us on this 16th day of May."

Longarm looked up. The four men stared back at him dumbfounded. Finally, Tom Hunter found his voice and said, "They'll never sign it."

Robert Goodman said, "That's a death warrant, Marshal. They're not going to sign that confession. Why should they?"

"For a lot of reasons. The main one being that I'm not going to take them straight to prison. Let me read this other document to you and maybe you'll understand how we're going to enforce this first one."

Hawkins said, "I'd damned sure like to see how you're going to enforce that first one. The minute you're gone, they'll be back up to their mischief."

Longarm said, "Just let me read you this." He picked up the second piece of paper.

"We the undersigned, Jake Myers and Archie Barrett, willingly and freely, agree to contribute $50,000 each to the Grit Settlement Association. This money will be held in a bank account in a bank in Junction, Texas, and will be administered by a committee of three, comprised of Tom Hunter, Robert Goodman, and Mrs. Milton Thompson. We understand that this money is to be used in several ways. First, it is to be used to make retribution to those who have suffered losses of property and life by our actions and at our hands. Secondly, this money will be used to make loans to those homesteaders who are having a hard time making a living because of our mischief, interference, and skullduggery. We further understand that if we commit any single act against any of the homesteaders that is to their harm, the confession we signed will immediately come into use and warrants will be issued for our arrest and we will be hunted down and brought to justice. We further understand that in one year from this date, we will each make an additional payment of $25,000 to the Grit Settlement Association. We each understand that the failure to do so will result in the publication of our confession and the issuance of warrants for our arrests. We understand that the confession we have given is not immediately being executed solely in order to repair the damage we have done to the settlement of Grit and to the innocent homesteaders who have tried to make a living here. We pledge ourselves to try our best to repair the damage we have done in the past, and we understand that is the sole reason we are not being taken into custody at the time we execute this document.

Signed by our hand on May 16.''

Longarm looked up. He said, ''Well?''

Hawkins found his voice first. He said, ''By damned, Marshal, that's slick. No question about it. In other words, you're holding out the carrot. If they behave themselves and don't cause no more trouble, you won't stick them in prison right away. But if they don't, they're going to prison right now.''

Longarm said, ''That's about the size of it, Mr. Hawkins. Or Deputy Hawkins as I should call you.''

Tom Hunter had an anxious look on his face. He said, ''Marshal, that's slick as bear grease, there's no question about it. But I just can't see them signing it. Why would they want to sign a confession?''

Robert Goodman said, ''Are you serious about this Grit Settlement Association? That's a wonderful idea. It's what Milton Thompson was trying to do. Lord knows, having money in the bank that we could borrow against would help a lot of families through these hard times.''

Longarm said, ''The way I look at it, Barrett and Myers did the damage, and I'm going to let them pay to repair it. Now, this ain't strictly going by the law, but then I never was much of one to go by the book. I ain't really got no way of proving anything against the two of them. They can get them a smart lawyer and they could play this thing out over several years and nothing would ever come of it. I figure if I could force them to sign these documents, some good would come out of it. Some people who have been hurt can start getting well. That's the way I see it.''

Tom Hunter said, ''It's a damned good idea, and it's a good way to do it. It's the right of the thing. I just hope to hell it will work, but I still can't see them signing this confession.''

Longarm said, ''Well, let's see. Bring them on out. We'll let them have a look and get their reaction. In fact, I think I'll let Deputy Hawkins here read it to them. Would you enjoy that, George?''

Hawkins chuckled his dry little sound. He said, ''Yeah, I reckon I would enjoy that. After all, that's lawmen's work.''

The difference between the two men was clearly obvious. Jake Myers was older, but Archie Barrett showed the effects of his confinement and ill use. It had obviously preyed on his mind. He looked wilted. He looked defeated. The thought crossed Longarm's mind that perhaps Jake Myers would have to undergo a few days of confinement himself before he could see a reason for signing the confession. He desperately hoped not. If there was any way he could wrap this business up and head back home, he would do it. Nothing he could think of would be more welcome than a train bound for Denver.

They both came in looking sullen and defiant, but there was still plenty of bluster in Jake Myers. Longarm listened to him spout and shout and curse for a moment or two. He turned to Tom Hunter. He said, ''Didn't I see a pair of good heavy leather work gloves around here?''

Hunter nodded. He said, ''They're out here on the back porch.''

''Would you kindly step out and hand them to me?''

''Be glad to.'' In a minute, he was back with the heavy rough leather gloves that had gauntlets that reached halfway up the forearms. Longarm took the pair, stepped deliberately over to the front of Jake Myers, and slapped him as hard as he could across the face with the gloves. The blow staggered the old man backward. A little blood came trickling from his lips.

155

Longarm said, "Now, listen you old bastard, you fucking murdering son of a bitch. You're here to listen. You keep your mouth shut until you're asked a question. If you say another word, you're going to get a lick of these gloves for every word you say. Have I made myself clear?"

Myers looked murderously at him. He said, "Yeah, I heard you."

Longarm slapped him with the gloves again, harder this time. "Didn't I tell you that you were going to get a lick for every word you said? You've got three more coming, by the way."

Some of the bluster had gone out of the old man. Now, he looked frightened.

Barrett said, "You're supposed to be a law officer. You ain't supposed to be hitting folks."

Longarm turned a gimlet eye on the man. He said, "Barrett, the same thing holds for you. Do you want a taste of these gloves, maybe with my fist in them?"

Archie Barrett turned his face and looked away.

Longarm went back around the table and sat down. He said, "Now, you two have been brought out here to hear something. I want you to listen to it, and then consider it very seriously." He turned to George Hawkins. He said, "Deputy Hawkins, would you read that first document? Just read the first one. Read it aloud and read it carefully so these dumb sons of bitches can understand it."

Longarm studied the two faces of his prisoners as Hawkins read with great delight the confession that Longarm wanted the men to sign. When he was finished, Barrett and Myers both exploded with a volley of curses. The main words they kept yelling over and over were, "Hell, no. Hell, no. We're not going to sign that damned thing. Do you think we're crazy?"

Longarm said, "Let's get something straight right now,

gentlemen. You don't have to sign that confession for me to have your ass. I can take you right outside to that old oak tree and hang you both for the evidence I've got on you."

Barrett said, bluster still in his voice, "You can't do no such thing."

Longarm said, "Mister, I'm afraid you've been misinformed. There is a law that says that a United States marshal, in the absence of a judge and jury, can take what steps he deems necessary to protect the public welfare. I think the public welfare would be well served by hanging the pair of you."

He was making it up out of whole cloth, but he doubted that they knew that.

His remark silenced both Barrett and Myers. They glanced at each other, looking worried. The other men in the room exchanged glances.

Longarm said, "But I don't want to do that. There is another way to handle this matter. As I have told these gentlemen, I am going to try and give y'all a chance to repair the damage you've done. Hanging you just gets rid of you. It doesn't pay back the widows, it doesn't rebuild the houses and the barns, it doesn't replace the cattle, and it doesn't get men back up on their feet that you have knocked down. Deputy, would you read the second document?"

Longarm leaned back in his chair and smoked a cigarillo while George Hawkins read the document about the Grit Settlement Association. When he was through, he could see that it had given Barrett and Myers food for thought, but Myers burst out, "Fifty thousand dollars? That's highway robbery! I'm not going to give you any fifty thousand dollars, not to save a bunch of tramps and bums. You're crazy as hell."

Longarm got up leisurely, picked up the gloves, and slapped the old man in the face again. Now his nose was starting to bleed. He said, "Myers, if you don't keep a civil tongue in your mouth, you ain't going to have a piece of skin left on your face."

He walked back to his chair at the table and sat down. He said, "Now, are you gentlemen willing to sign these documents?"

Archie Barrett said, "I ain't. I ain't signing no confession to murder. You must think I'm crazy."

Myers said, "I ain't either."

Longarm nodded his head. He said, "Throw them back in their room, boys. And would y'all please quit being so gentle? You're just too nice to these fellows."

As the Goodmans and Tom Hunter were shoving the two prisoners back to the small stone room, George Hawkins looked over at Longarm and cackled his dry laugh. He said, "You're about half mean, ain't you, Marshal?"

Longarm said, "That hurts my feelings."

"What? Calling you mean?"

"Yeah, I don't like that half part."

Hawkins cackled again. He said, "I've got a feeling, though, this ain't your regular style."

Longarm shrugged. "You don't play every hand of poker the same, do you?"

"No, indeed," Hawkins said. "Every card is different."

"Well, these are two of the worst cards I've ever run into and I don't figure anything is too bad for them."

Hawkins said, "You really think they're going to sign that confession?"

"If they don't, they're going to wish they had, before it's all over. I'll take them into custody and I'll make up evidence if I have to."

Hawkins looked at him strangely. "You'd do that?"

Longarm took a draw of his cigarillo and blew the smoke into the air. "In this case, yeah. That is, if I don't have to shoot them escaping. There's always that chance."

Hawkins looked at Longarm curiously. He said, "You know, Marshal, I've played poker with you and you're a hard man to figure out if you're bluffing. Right now, I don't know if you're bluffing or not about all this."

Longarm shrugged again and gave him a smile. He said, "If you can figure out it's a bluff, then it's not much of a bluff, now, is it? I always found out the best hand to bluff with was four aces."

They brought the two men out again that night about eight o'clock, well after supper. Neither had been given food or drink. By now, Barrett knew what that meant. Jake Myers was just starting to find out, and he complained loud and hard about the treatment. All he received in return was silence.

Longarm said, "You boys ready to sign yet?"

Barrett said, "Hell, no. I ain't ready to put no rope around my neck."

"The same goes for me," said Myers.

Longarm nodded. He said, "Well, welcome back to the Hardship Hotel. Show them back to their room, boys."

They stood watch again that night. With five of them, they were two beds short, so Rufus made himself a pallet on the cold stone floor and did the best he could. His daddy said it wouldn't bother him. He said, "That boy can sleep standing up if there's any work around."

Longarm caught the watch just before dawn. He was making the coffee when the others began to stir. Tom Hunter came in to help. He said, "I'm getting worried. There'll be scouting parties out looking for both of them by now. I would think that one ranch has talked to the other ranch, and they've found out that both of the big shots are missing. I think we can expect some trouble real soon."

Longarm said, "I hope so. It's been pretty dull around here."

Tom Hunter looked at Longarm. He said, "You actually like it when the guns are going off?"

Longarm shook his head. He said, "No, but at least I know that some progress is being made in one direction or another."

They let the cabin fill with the smell of frying meat and eggs and biscuits before they brought the two prisoners back in. Both of them were all eyes for the kitchen. Both of them looked wan and dried. Jake Myers, especially, looked drawn out and tired. Longarm put the same question to each of them. The answer was the same.

This time, Longarm put his boots up on a handy chair and folded his hands up behind his neck. He said, "Gentlemen, I don't think you fully understand your options. Now, if you do this like I've laid it out for you, you're going to be able to walk out of here free. That is, so long as you keep your part about the money. I'll have the confessions, and I'll execute them when and if you get out of line again. But for the time being, you are going to be as free as a bird."

Barrett looked at Myers and the older man looked back. Jake Myers said, "I don't trust you, Marshal, any further than I can throw a wagon load of manure. If we sign those confessions, then you're going to drag us off to jail."

Longarm brought his feet to the floor with a thump. He said, "Jake, you don't know it, but I can drag you off to jail and probably have you in prison inside of three months and maybe get you hung. In fact, I might could just take you outside right now and hang you. I'm offering you a chance. You don't seem to understand that."

Myers said, "Well, I ain't signing no document."

Longarm nodded his head and made a motion, and once again, the complaining prisoners were taken back to their room without food or water.

Hawkins said, "They're a blamed sight harder and more

stubborn than I thought they'd be. Hell, Barrett ain't had but one meal in about three days. Of course, Jake Myers could live off his fat for some time. But I would imagine that things are beginning to pinch both of them a little. Do you mean what you say about them being free if they sign that document?''

''Yeah, I mean it. As I've tried to explain it, I'm just trying to bring some peace to this place. Get things working again.''

It was in the afternoon, about three o'clock, that Rufus spotted scouts roaming through the countryside. He called Longarm over to one of the windows and the marshal looked out. He could see a few riders working the ground between the eastern side and back toward town. They were a good two or three miles from the cabin, but at any time, one or more could present themselves.

At about four o'clock, Longarm had the two men brought back out for what he told them would be the last question of the day. He said, ''This is about the last time I'm going to ask you. We're going to start fixing supper pretty soon, and we're either going to put your names in the pot now, or they're not going in at all. The next time you're going to be asked this question, it's going to be tomorrow morning, after breakfast, and after another night without any water or any food. So, I'm going to ask you one more time what you're willing to do. Are you willing to sign these confessions?''

Before they could answer, young Rufus yelled from a front window, ''Marshal! Marshal! There's a big body of men headed straight this way.''

Longarm stood up, but even as he did, Archie Barrett made a bolt for the door. Longarm would have never thought he could have moved so fast as he did after being starved down for several days and deprived of water. He was out the door before anyone could touch him.

Robert Goodman was moving even faster. He was out the

door right behind Barrett and within three steps had wrestled him to the ground. By the time Longarm reached the door, Goodman was jerking the struggling rancher back toward the rock house. But the biggest sight was a party of at least two dozen men coming up the slope toward the cabin. They were only some three hundred yards away.

Longarm said quickly, "Throw them back into the room. Get your rifles and get to the windows and let's start pouring some fire into that bunch before they scatter."

Chapter 10

At first, they could bring only two rifles to bear on the large, advancing party: Longarm's and that of young Rufus. Hawkins was firing, too; but as he freely admitted, he would have been better off chucking rocks. Mr. Goodman and Tom Hunter were meanwhile occupied trying to get the struggling prisoners back into their room of confinement. They had been delayed because Jake Myers had tried to escape, as Barrett had, making a run for freedom through the front.

Longarm, firing fast, was able to hit at least three men or their horses, and he could tell that Rufus's fire was also doing damage. They had forced the men to split up and disperse into a long line. Most of them had quit their horses and were advancing on foot, which made them harder to hit. By the time Robert Goodman and Tom Hunter had taken their positions, Longarm could tell they were in trouble because the long line of gunmen were going to flank the cabin on both sides, and they didn't have enough firepower to defend from each side.

For a moment or two, he had been concentrating on each end of the line, forcing those that would approach the cabin from the ends to fall back. He had estimated that they had dropped six or seven of the two dozen attackers, but there were still too many of them left to handle. He didn't know if they were Myers's men or Barrett's men or a mixture of both. Neither did Tom Hunter or either of the Goodmans.

Robert Goodman said, "It's too far, Marshal. I can't pick out the faces. They're starting to get to cover behind those little rocky ledges down there. They're going to make this place get kind of warm."

The words were no sooner out of his mouth than bullets began to come in through the windows and richochet off the stone walls. Longarm was firing from a corner near the front door. He said, "Everybody keep down. I'm going to try to keep them the least bit busy here. Tom, you and Mr. Goodman go fetch Barrett and Myers. We've got to do something quick before we get drilled three or four times by the same bullet ricocheting around this room. Damn! There's good things to be said about a stone house, but there's also some bad things to be said. They'll keep the bullets out, but if they get in, they'll damned sure bounce around."

Firing as fast as he could and reloading his rifle from the cartridges in his shirt pocket, Longarm was able to keep the return rifle fire to a minimum and also keep each end of the advancing line from flanking him. He knew that such tactics weren't going to last long. Behind him, he heard a sudden cry and looked to his left. Young Rufus Goodman was squatting in the corner. He had his hand pressed to his right shoulder. Longarm could see blood. Longarm said, "Son, are you hurt?"

There was pain on the young man's face. He said through

gritted teeth, "Not so you'd notice. It just got meat, no bone. I'll be all right." With that, he stood up and fired three quick shots through the open window and then hunkered back down again.

There were still shells coming through the door and the window and the ones that didn't bury themselves into the table or a chair bounced at least twice. It made it very dangerous to be standing up in the room. Hawkins was at the right-hand window. He'd pulled a chair over and was sort of wearing it like a turtle back. From time to time, he stood up and blindly fired a shot.

Longarm said, "Quit wasting that ammunition, George. You ain't hit anything. I don't think that last shot even hit the world, or at least in this county. Stay down under that chair. We might need you again."

Longarm fired two quick shots and he saw one man suddenly stand up and fall backward. He calculated that they had depleted the ranks of their attackers by at least seven or eight men.

Just then, Hunter and Robert Goodman came out, prodding Barrett and Myers ahead of them. Tom Hunter said, "Here they are, Marshal."

Longarm waved frantically. He said, "Get them over here in the door."

Myers said, "You go to hell, Mr. son-of-a-bitch Marshal. Now, you're going to get yours. You're going to see what it's like."

Longarm said, "Get in this door."

Barrett said, "We ain't going to do no such thing." Just then, two slugs came whining through the left-hand window, struck the far wall, ricocheted off another wall, and then off the back wall and then off the floor and buried themselves in the ceiling. Both slugs passed within a foot of Barrett and Myers.

165

Longarm gave them a lean smile. He said, "All right, gentlemen. Just stand right where you are and you're fixing to get hemstitched by about a dozen slugs from your own men."

Myers suddenly moved, heading for the door. Barrett was right behind him. Longarm stood up, pressing his back against the wooden door. He grabbed each man and turned and stopped them right at the door. He shoved the Winchester into Myers's back. He said, "Both of you, wave your arms. Start yelling for them to stop firing. Do it right now, or so help me, I'll blow a hole through your kidney."

Barrett and Myers both raised their arms and waved and took turns shouting, "Stop shooting! Hold your fire! Stop!"

Gradually, the firing stopped. The silence slowly became total. It sounded eerie inside the cabin where there had been so many explosions and so many twanging sounds from the slugs.

Archie Barrett looked back over his shoulder at Longarm and bared his teeth. He said, "Well now, Marshal. It looks like we've got you."

"You ain't looked real good, Mr. Barrett. This rifle of mine is pointed straight at you, and you ain't going anywhere. You try to move, and you will be shot escaping."

Jake Myers said, "Yeah, but you're surrounded now, and you ain't going nowhere."

Longarm said, "They're not going to shoot in here, not unless you want to get killed. Tell them to back off two or three hundred yards—they're way too close. We need to have a talk, us three, so you yell down there, both of you, and tell them to back up."

Barrett said, "What if we don't?"

Longarm slapped him on the side of his head with the barrel of his rifle. He said, "If you don't, it ain't going to get pleasant. I'm willing for you to stand there in that door for the rest of your life. Now, if you want to talk, tell those men to back off."

Reluctantly, both men, yelling and pushing with their hands, directed the men that worked for each of them to pull back. Each time they stopped, Longarm would say, "Farther." Finally, they were a good four or five hundred yards away. He said, "They can sit down now. You two gentlemen can get back in here in this cabin."

Tom Hunter and Mr. Goodman grabbed Barrett and Myers and jerked them back inside the cabin.

Mr. Goodman said, "What do we do with them? Shove them back in that room?"

Longarm shook his head. "No, we're pretty near the time for a showdown. Set them down at the table. Either they're going to sign now or they ain't ever going to sign. I'll be right with you."

Longarm took the time to pour himself a glass of whiskey, very conscious that Barrett and Myers were both watching him, the desire for the whiskey clear in their eyes. He came over to the table and then sat down. He motioned for Tom Hunter to put both the confession and the terms of agreement for the Grit Settlement Association in front of the two men.

He took a slow sip of the whiskey and then took time to light a cigarillo. When he finished doing that, he said, "Now, let's examine the situation. You think you've got me because you've got some hired hands out there. What are you paying them? Eighty dollars a month? One hundred dollars a month? One hundred and fifty dollars a month? Probably some of them are kinfolk, but that doesn't matter. They've already seen that over a half dozen of their number have been killed, along with the number that I've killed on my own. You ain't going to buy a man's life for what you're paying them. Pretty soon, they're going to get tired of watching this rock cabin and waiting to see what we're going to do. I know one thing that you're not going to do, and that is walk out of here until you sign these documents. Now, my deal is real simple. You sign this confession and you keep the peace, and I give you my word that that'll be the end of it. You sign it and break the peace, and I'll give you my word that I'll cover you up with marshals and United States calvary and anything else it takes to hang you from the nearest tree. You break even one part of this settlement agreement, and you'll rue the day. Sign it, keep the peace, and walk free. Don't sign it, and there's a damned good chance of getting killed while I take you to prison. You've got two places you're going if you don't sign these papers, and that's to the funeral parlor or to a federal prison. You can make up your mind, either way.''

Barrett still wanted to bluster. ''Yeah, but you'll never get out of here alive. None of you.''

Longarm smiled. He said, ''You want to bet your life on that?''

Suddenly, Jake Myers caved in. He heaved a big sigh. He said, ''Is this all you want? We sign these and we're free?''

''If you keep your word.''

Barrett said, ''Yeah, but will you keep yours with that confession?''

Longarm said, ''Mr. Barrett, you haven't known me long enough for me to take offense to that statement. Otherwise, I'd knock you out of that chair. If I tell you I'll keep my word, you can believe it. If I tell you a jackrabbit can pull a freight train, you might as well go ahead and hook it up because the jackrabbit can. I've made it all clear to you. Are y'all a little thick-headed or what? So, here's the papers. Sign them or not. You've got one minute.''

Jake Myers looked at Barrett and shrugged. He said, ''I don't see where we got a choice. If we don't sign the confession, he's going to make up evidence, anyway. We can't go on doing business with him making a mess of things here.

What good's the confession, anyway? We've got lawyers. If he tries to use it, we can give him a hell of a fight. But I can't take much more of this kind of living. I'm too old for it." He reached for the pen, dipped it in the ink, and signed it Jake L. Myers.

Barrett thought for a moment and then he took the pen from Myers's hand and signed the confession just under the signature of the other man. Longarm took the pen from him and dipped it back into the ink and then held it out for Tom Hunter. He said, "Each of you sign as witnesses."

One by one, they wrote their signatures. Longarm finished the confession by writing:

Given into my hand this 16th day of May, willingly, by Archie Barrett and Jake Myers and witnessed by the above.

Then he took the confession, folded it carefully once he was sure the ink was dry, and buttoned it into his shirt pocket. After that, he put the agreement for the Settlement Association in front of the two men. He said, "Now this."

Mr. Myers looked annoyed. He said, "Hell, that's a lot of money. Fifty thousand dollars."

Longarm looked over at Tom Hunter. He said, "Tom, how much money do you reckon these settlers have been robbed of by these two scoundrels?"

Tom Hunter shrugged. He said, "I couldn't count it, but it's a hell of a lot more than fifty thousand dollars apiece. Besides, how do you put a price on a cabin that a man built with his own hand and how do you put a price on a man's life? How do you put a price on how a wife feels when she loses a husband? Or the children?"

Longarm held the pen out to Jake Myers. He said, "Sign it."

Myers sighed, dipped the pen, and wrote his name and

handed the pen to Archie Barrett. Barrett didn't even hesitate. In a tired hand, he scrawled his name.

Once again, Longarm had each of the men present, including Hawkins, witness the document, and as before, he wrote at the bottom that he, as an official of the United States government, had received the document into his hand at such a time and on such a date.

Archie Barrett looked up at him. He said, "Now, is that it?"

"Not quite." Longarm shook his head.

Barrett said, "I ain't doing another damned thing until I get some food and some whiskey."

"Your job ain't done yet, Barrett," Longarm said. "Remember, you've got to get fifty thousand dollars over to a bank in Junction. Did you bring your checkbook with you?"

Barrett looked furious. "Whether I've got my checkbook with me is none of your affair."

Hawkins said, "Oh, he's got his checkbook, all right, Marshal. I saw him special put it in his pocket, thinking he could buy that saddle of that assassinated president of Mexico. Yeah, he's got it. I bet if you go in there and look in his jacket, you'd find it."

Barrett looked livid. "You better not touch my personal belongings! As it happens, I do have a checkbook, but it's not on an account that I've got that kind of money in."

"Then you both better send to your headquarters, and you both better get a check, because you ain't getting out of here until an account gets open in Junction with one hundred thousand dollars in it. Now, is that clear? And you ain't going to get a bite to eat or a drop to drink until I see those checks on the way. You *comprende, hombres?*"

Jake Myers was looking more and more tired. He said, "How are we supposed to get our drafts—"

Longarm interrupted. He said, "I suggest you send one of

your men back to each of your places and have him locate wherever you keep your checkbook and have him get on back here. That's the fastest way, as far as I'm concerned.''

They both shrugged. Jake Myers said, ''Why not?'' He turned around in his chair and looked out the door. ''I think my son James is out there. If he is, one of you call for him.''

Longarm looked at Barrett. He said, ''What about you?''

''Any of my men will do. I know that neither one of my brothers are out there, but they can give him the checkbook. Just call for one of my men.''

''I think you had better do that,'' Longarm said. ''Stand there in the door in case anybody's got an itchy trigger finger. Call for James Myers and for whoever you want.''

Barrett stood up. He said to the marshal, ''You think you've won, but you might yet regret this.''

Longarm smiled. ''Oh, I generally regret everything I do. But the funny thing about it is that the other fellow usually regrets it more. Now, get busy.''

Within half an hour, two men had been dispatched to both ranches to fetch back the checkbooks. Archie Barrett said, ''Now, I want some food and a drink of whiskey.''

Longarm said, ''There's only one last thing, Mr. Barrett, and I'm sure you won't mind doing this since it's for your own good.'' He turned to Tom Hunter. ''Tom, would you give me two more pieces of paper?''

While he was waiting for the paper, he turned to George Hawkins and said, ''Mr. Hawkins, what's one of your top saddles?''

Hawkins thought for a moment. ''Well, I reckon that would be the Cheyenne model. It's a double girthed, deep seated saddle with a high roping pommel. Comes with a matching breastplate.''

''What does it sell for?''

"We generally sell it, shipping charges included, for around one hundred and forty-five dollars."

"Good." Longarm took the two pieces of paper and wrote out an order for ten saddles to be bought by Mr. Myers and ten saddles to be bought by Mr. Barrett. He handed Mr. Myers the pen and said, "You just bought ten saddles. My deputy has been put to some considerable trouble on your account, and I think he ought to be compensated."

Myers looked up at him with rage in his eyes that slowly dissolved to resignation. He signed the order and then shoved it away from him. In a moment, Archie Barrett did the same. Longarm took the two orders and turned around and handed them to George Hawkins, who cackled in glee.

Longarm said, "See, you tell me that the law business don't pay? Why sure and you'll get your two dollars a day on top of that."

Hawkins said, "Well, you never did explain it to me that way before. If you had explained it before, I would have just volunteered."

"Volunteered? You wouldn't have volunteered, George, if I had thrown in a velvet easy chair to go with it."

An hour later, Tom Hunter and the two Goodmans were riding for Junction with the two checks in hand. Longarm's instructions to them had been simple. There would be three people who would sign each check: Tom Hunter, Robert Goodman, and Mrs. Thompson. Before they had left, he had promised Myers and Barrett what would happen to them if there was any problem with the checks. He said, "You don't want to find out, that I promise you."

But all that was over now, and the Settlement Association was well on its way to being a working institution. Longarm said to Jake Myers and Archie Barrett, "Now, all right. Get your gear, get your clothes, and get anything else you've left here, including your stink, and get the hell out of here. Take those men down the hill with you. And you better hope that I don't see either one of you again, because if I do, it's going to be for the purpose of killing you. Understand me?''

Neither man would look at him. Meyers never had gotten any food, and Longarm had said, ''You certainly ain't going to get any of my whiskey. I barely will allow close friends to share that. You can imagine just how much chance you've got.''

Now there was no one left but Longarm and Hawkins. Together, they gathered up their gear and walked across the floor that was littered with brass cartridge cases. They went out, saddled their horses, and started the slow ride to town.

Hawkins said, as they started down the hill, ''You know, Longarm, sometimes the leather business gets a little dull. It kind of does a man good to get some excitement in his life every once in a while.''

''George, what do you think Mrs. Thompson is going to think about all this?''

''I think she'll be right pleased. If we hurry along, we should get there in time for supper, and you can tell her all about it.''

Longarm said, ''We'll both tell her about it. You had a big hand in this, George. I'm going to see to it that you get a medal and two dollars a day.''

''How many days I got coming?''

''Oh, three.''

Hawkins shook his head. ''Six whole dollars. I don't have any idea what I'll do with that kind of money.''

Longarm said, ''You could lose it to me playing poker.''

''No, it's too hard. It's hard to lose to you, Marshal.''

Longarm gave him an eye. He said, ''You're liable to talk yourself into losing a little more than six dollars if you're not careful.''

Hawkins was silent for a time. Then, as they neared town, he said, "You know, Marshal, that was about the slickest way out of that mess I could have imagined. How did you ever think of a way to do that so that it would kind of make the best out of a bad situation?"

Longarm laughed slightly. He said, "George, it wasn't so much that I thought that up. It was just that I couldn't think of anything else. It happened by kind of a process of elimination, you might say."

"Well, it worked out for the best. You reckon they'll keep to their end of the bargain?"

Longarm looked at him and said grimly, "I know I will. If they make one little slip, they're going to wish they had never been born."

Chapter 11

It took several more days to see to the setting up of the Grit Settlement Association. Word spread like wildfire, and the town was soon thronged with people who had been struggling on small farms and ranches. They clogged and crowded Mrs. Thompson's boardinghouse until rules had to be established. Longarm presided over the rule-making and the installation of the officers. After that, it was out of his hands. The board consisted of Robert Goodman, Tom Hunter, and Mrs. Thompson, with Mrs. Thompson serving as president of the board. It was a bold move for a woman to have the deciding vote, but it seemed only fitting in view of what her husband had attempted. In many ways, the Grit Settlement Association was framed and formed on his ideas. During this time, Hawkins reluctantly took his leave. Longarm wrote him a letter stating that he had served honorably for a week as an auxiliary deputy United States marshal and that George

Hawkins was entitled to all emoluments and courtesies due that rank.

Hawkins looked the paper. He said, "What's an emolument?"

Longarm shook his head. "I don't know, but they always put that word in them kind of documents. As far as I know, it means you get the cream with the milk. But if you ever do run across an emolument, I wish you'd get in touch with me and let me know."

They shook hands, and Hawkins departed. Longarm doubted that he would ever see the man again, but then that was the way with so much of his work. He met people and became so close to them under the intense pressure and danger of situations, and then it was all over with and everyone went their own way. Just as he now was anxiously looking forward to finishing up and leaving Grit and leaving Texas and getting back home to Denver.

His work was finally done and he would be going the next day. That night, he sat in his room on the side of his bed, thinking and having one last drink and smoking a cigarillo. He thought about Billy Vail and what he had told him about the circus. Well, he had been right. This was the damnedest bunch of lions and tigers he had ever seen. He hadn't been sure how he was going to tame them without a whip and a chair.

Since he was fixing to go to bed, he wasn't wearing any clothes. He had the lamp trimmed down low because it was just before he was to extinguish it. Longarm guessed it was going on midnight. He would pick up his train the next day somewhere around noon, so there was no rush. As long as he was out of Grit by nine o'clock, he'd have plenty of time to catch the little rattle-banger that ran between Junction and Brady.

As he was sitting there thinking back over the past time

and all that had happened, there came a very light tap at his door. Without thinking, he said, "Come in."

The door opened slowly and Mrs. Thompson came softly into the room. Longarm was so startled, he almost stood up. She was wearing a pale pink nightgown of very sheer material. He could see that she had fixed her hair and put on some rouge and touched up her lips and eyes. It was clearly obvious what she had come for.

He made no attempt to hide his nakedness. He said, "Mrs. Thompson, are you sure about this?"

She moved toward him, holding out her hand to touch his face as she did. She said, "Yes. Very sure. I've held myself alone and without long enough."

Longarm said, "I know you set a great deal of store by your husband."

"Yes," she said, "and I still do. But this is different. You did a wonderful thing here. What you did for these people, the help you gave them, the peace that you brought back to this area, the prosperity."

Longarm said, his voice going husky, "Well, I don't need any thanks, ma'am. It's my job."

"This is not thanks. This is what I want to do, that is, if you want to."

"Oh, ma'am. Yes, I want to very much. I'm just surprised, that's all. You've kind of taken me off guard."

She said, "Let me get in the bed."

Longarm scooted back on the bed to make room for her, but before she moved forward, she lifted her nightgown over her head and then stood there for a moment. The sight made the breath catch in Longarm's throat. She was not some young shapely girl who, in spite of her looks, had not had the experience that radiated from Mrs. Thompson's mature body. There was a fullness about it, a voluptuousness and experience that could only come with maturity. Her breasts were full and round. They hung a little, but then they had been used. Her hips were wider than they would have been ten years before, and her belly was rounder, but the way the lamplight glanced off the sheen of her skin and the high points of her body caused Longarm's breath to come faster and faster. He fastened his eyes on the vee of black, rich pubic hair that was almost at the level of his eyes. He let his gaze travel up to her breasts, to her face, and then to her hair. He held out his hand. She reached and took it, and he pulled her to him. They came slowly together.

For half an hour, they made slow, preparatory, teasing, flattering love play. Then, when she was ready, Longarm brought her to climax with finger and tongue and penis. He held her while she shuddered and screamed softly into his neck. She had her legs locked around his hips and with strong pulls, she drove him deeper into herself. In three or four rhythmic plunges, he erupted and filled her with semen in a long, slow, star-bursting cascade of tingling satisfaction. When it was over, he collapsed on her for a moment and then rolled to the side and lay next to her.

Neither one of them spoke for a few long moments. Finally she said, "Well, first Milton ruins me for other men, and now you come along. What am I supposed to do?"

Longarm said, "Just judging from what I've seen of him, Robert Goodman appears to be a good man." He realized what he had said and then laughed. "I guess he would have to be a good man, wouldn't he?"

"I've been watching him. He's interesting, he's steady, he's not too imaginative, but I think I could always depend on him."

Longarm said, "I think so. I think he's the kind of man who would wear well, like Tom Hunter."

She turned her head toward him. "Or like you?"

He shook his head. "No, ma'am. I'm not here for the long haul. It just ain't in the cards for me."

"You could never marry?"

Longarm said, "I don't see how. It would be unfair to both parties. It would be unfair to the woman because I'd be gone all the time, and it would be unfair to me because I might be thinking of her at the wrong time and be just that fraction of a second too slow. No, ma'am, I'm here to do a job and then I'll go someplace else to do a job." He turned and propped his head on his elbow. "But I won't soon forget this night. Ma'am, you're a wonderful, lovely woman. You give a man great pleasure. I'd say that if I wanted or if I had to choose one woman to sleep with for the rest of my life, your name would be well up near the top of the list."

She smiled in the dim glow of the lantern. She said, "And I'm sure that's quite a list. But I am complimented and I thank you for everything that you did. You're leaving in the morning?"

Longarm nodded. "Yep, I'll probably be out of here around nine."

"Tomorrow, I'll be Mrs. Thompson, the landlady of the boardinghouse, so I'll only bid you good-bye like that. But I'd still like to give you a real good-bye tonight." She reached out her arms and drew his head slowly toward her lips. He went willingly.

Longarm was less than two hours out of Denver and thoroughly tired of train travel, but he felt a great sense of satisfaction with the job he had just done. It had been an unusual job, much different than his ordinary line of work. He had left two criminals in place, but he had made the judgment, and he still felt it was the right one. If they went wrong on him, then he was going to come down on them like a ton of bricks. He thought he had taken the law and applied it to the best interests of the most people.

He stretched and yawned and took a nip out of the bottle of whiskey he had on the seat beside him. It was going to be good to get home, even if Billy Vail was going to be there and would be trying to get him out of town as soon as possible. His mind turned for a moment to Mrs. Thompson, but then he turned it away. Women like Mrs. Thompson weren't for him. Her kind didn't come along very often. She was best left as a wonderful memory.

Longarm yawned again and wondered if the young lady named Betty Shaw would still be in town when he got home. If she was, maybe she'd help him wash the trail dust off himself. But if not her, then maybe the dressmaker lady. All in all, it had been a good job, and he felt content.

Watch for

LONGARM AND THE CRYING CORPSE

219th novel in the bold LONGARM series
from Jove

Coming in March!

If you enjoyed this book, subscribe now and get...

TWO FREE

A $7.00 VALUE—

If you would like to read more of the very best, most exciting, adventurous, action-packed Westerns being published today, you'll want to subscribe to True Value's Western Home Subscription Service.

Each month the editors of True Value will select the 6 very best Westerns from America's leading publishers for special readers like you. You'll be able to preview these new titles as soon as they are published, *FREE* for ten days with no obligation!

TWO FREE BOOKS

When you subscribe, we'll send you your first month's shipment of the newest and best 6 Westerns for you to preview. With your first shipment, two of these books will be yours as our introductory gift to you absolutely *FREE* (a $7.00 value), regardless of what you decide to do. If

you like them, as much as we think you will, keep all six books but pay for just 4 at the low subscriber rate of just $2.75 each. If you decide to return them, keep 2 of the titles as our gift. No obligation.

Special Subscriber Savings

When you become a True Value subscriber you'll save money several ways. First, all regular monthly selections will be billed at the low subscriber price of just $2.75 each. That's at least a savings of $4.50 each month below the publishers price. Second, there is never any shipping, handling or other hidden charges—*Free home delivery*. What's more there is no minimum number of books you must buy, you may return any selection for full credit and you can cancel your subscription at any time. A TRUE VALUE!

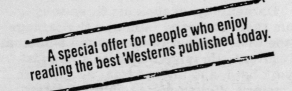